The Mystery of
Claw Mountain

The Mystery Series
Book 4

The Mystery of Claw Mountain

PAUL MOXHAM

Copyright

CONTENTS

CHAPTER 1

SCOTLAND

Joe Mitchell opened his eyes. The morning sun was streaming through the bedroom window and for a moment he wondered where he was. As he sat up, he saw Will sleeping in the bed beside him. He grinned as he remembered the events of the last few days.

Although he had enjoyed spending his summer holidays at the seaside village of Smugglers Cove, he'd been thrilled when his parents had asked him and his sisters if they'd like to spend a week in Scotland with their grandparents.

Knowing how downhearted their best friend would be if they weren't spending the Christmas holiday's with him at Smugglers Cove, Joe had asked Will if he wanted to accompany them. He had said yes, so things were quickly put into motion.

Will had listened with interest as Mrs Mitchell explained to him that ever since Grandpa Mitchell had retired, he and his wife had been looking for a country property that they could move to. On a trip to Scotland last year they had seen Heather Hills, a small farm, and had immediately fallen in love with it. Wild heather grew on the surrounding slopes and a craggy mountain rose up into the sky behind it. They had both thought it looked magical.

The drive up to Scotland had been long, but it hadn't been dreary. At least not for Joe. He had gazed out of the window for most of the trip and had been disappointed when night had fallen. He had been hoping to have a look at the farm in the light of day but, by the time the car had turned into the driveway, daylight was long gone.

Remembering that it had been lightly snowing when he had stepped out of the car, Joe climbed out of bed and hurried to the window.

He grinned. There was a clear blue sky and the entire landscape was completely covered in snow.

As he gazed out, he imagined all the fun they were going to have while they were staying here. He had once seen snow in London, but nowhere near as much as this. Hearing a noise, Joe glanced around and saw Will sitting up.

The boy yawned loudly and brushed a lock of red hair out of his eyes. "Is it still snowing?"

Joe shook his head. "No, but there's more snow out there than we'll ever want. We'll be able to go tobogganing—"

"And have a snowball fight," Will interrupted.

"And go ice skating." Joe peered through the window once more as he attempted to see the pond that his grandfather had talked about the previous night, but the barn hid it from view.

Will yawned. "I wonder if the girls are awake yet."

"I'll go and see." Joe hurried to the door and opened it. As he stepped out of the room, the sound of voices downstairs greeted him, but he couldn't make out who they belonged too. He padded across the carpeted hallway and knocked on the door. "Amy! Sarah! Are you awake?"

There was no response, so he went downstairs. The voices were coming from the kitchen so he headed in that direction.

As Joe walked into the room, he was surprised to see his parents and his sisters, Amy and Sarah, having breakfast. "Golly, I must have slept longer than I thought."

"Well, we did have a big drive yesterday," Mr Mitchell replied, glancing up at Joe and smiling. "And this is a holiday, so you can get up whatever time you want."

"But the longer I stay in bed, the less time I'll have time to do stuff." Joe looked at the girls. "Did you see all the snow?"

Sarah beamed in delight. "Yes. I can't wait to go out."

"Nor me," Joe replied. "How about we go outside straight after breakfast?"

"Yes, let's," Sarah said.

"You'd better go and wake Will then," Amy suggested.

Joe hurried upstairs and, before long, he and Will were eating a hearty breakfast that his grandmother had cooked for them. Joe glanced around. "Hey, where's Jock?"

Amy looked around the kitchen. "I'm not sure. He was in here earlier."

Just then his grandmother walked in. She was a plump woman with short brown hair that was starting to turn grey. She had a round cheery face and was wearing a blue and white checked apron.

"Do you know where Jock is?" Joe asked.

"I think he followed Arthur to the woodpile." Grandma peered out of the window and smiled. "Yes, there he is."

"I was surprised to hear you had got another dog," Amy said. "I didn't think you were planning on buying another one after Rover died."

Her grandmother sat down at the table. "No, we weren't, but…" She gazed down at the floor for a moment. "I'd better start at the beginning. One cold, wet day about six weeks ago, we were sitting by the fire when we heard a dog whimpering. We went to the front door and there was this poor, thin, bedraggled creature. He was shivering uncontrollably, and when we opened the door he ran inside. He was such a pathetic sight we didn't have the heart to put him outside. We got some old towels and dried him off by the fire. He was so thin you could see his ribs. When we gave him some food he gobbled it down as though he hadn't seen any for weeks."

"Then what did you do?" Amy asked, captivated by the story.

"Well, we put up notices all around Dunmoore, but a week later, when no one had responded to them, we decided we would adopt him." Grandma paused as she heard the front door open. She waited for a moment and called out. "Jock!"

The children listened and smiled in anticipation as they heard a pattering of footsteps. A few moments later, a large brown dog ran into the kitchen.

Grandma lovingly stroked his head as the children stood up and crowded around the animal. One by one, the children said hello to the dog and patted him. Jock responded with a sloppy tongue on their faces.

Amy couldn't keep the smile off her face as she hugged Jock. She loved all animals, but she especially loved dogs. She turned to her grandmother. "I can see why you love him."

Joe looked up as his grandfather entered the kitchen and went to wash his hands at the sink. He too was on the plump side and had grey hair and grey-blue eyes. He smiled at the children. "I see you like Jock."

"He seems nice," Joe said.

Grandpa suddenly became serious. "You might not believe it, but I think Jock has a sixth sense."

"Sixth sense?" Sarah frowned. "What's a sixth sense?"

"Well, you know how you can see, touch, feel, hear and smell?" Grandpa replied. As the girl nodded, the man resumed speaking. "Well, that's five senses. I believe Jock has all those, but also another one."

Will frowned. "What do you mean?"

"Well, he can sense things," Grandpa said. "Things that we don't even know about."

"What things?" Amy asked, intrigued.

"Shortly after Jock arrived, I was over in the woods collecting pine cones for the fire," Grandpa explained. "I carelessly stepped into a badger hole and twisted my ankle so badly I couldn't walk. I yelled for help and, when no one came to my rescue, I decided to call Jock's name. I didn't imagine it would do any good, since I thought he was sitting in front of the warm fire. But, lo and behold, five minutes later there he was, smothering me with licks. I told him to go and get help."

"And did he?" Sarah asked.

Grandpa nodded. "He sure did. And for that I'm very grateful. I'm not sure how long I would have been stuck there if Jock hadn't come along."

"Maybe he was nearby somewhere," Will said. "Maybe that's how he could hear you."

"He was sitting beside me by the fire." Grandma shared a glance with her husband and then turned to the children. "So, either he has exceptional hearing or else he can sense when someone is in trouble."

"That's an amazing story," Amy said.

"Yes, it is." Grandma stood up. "I'd better get started on the dishes. Now, do you children want more toast?"

CHAPTER 2

HEATHER HILLS

Half an hour later, dressed in coats, gloves, scarves, hats, and boots, the four children left the warmth of the farmhouse and stepped out into the crisp morning air.

Joe turned to the others. "Shall we have a look at the toboggans that Grandpa said were in the barn? Then we can explore the rest of the farm."

Sarah, the youngest of the four children, nodded. "I wonder if Jock wants to come outside and have a walk with us."

"I'll go and get him." Amy walked back into the farmhouse and yelled out. "Jock! Jock!" For a moment there was silence, and then the brown dog bounded down the hallway. Amy smiled and patted him. "Come on boy, let's go outside."

Inside the barn were several bales of hay and a large stack of firewood. Joe was the first to spy the toboggans and ice skates that were stacked in one corner. He raced over to them. "The toboggans look fairly old."

Amy knelt down and examined one of the toboggans "Apart from being a bit dirty and dusty, they look fine."

"When shall we test them out?" Sarah asked.

"Later today," Joe said.

Amy picked up one of the pairs of skates. "Grandma told me that, after she heard that all four of us were coming up for Christmas, she and Grandpa went shopping and bought these skates for us to use."

As each of them found a pair that seemed to be the right size, they quickly took off their boots and tried them on.

Sarah's green eyes shone with delight as she finished putting on the skates she had chosen. "They fit perfectly!"

"I think mine do too." Amy looked over at Joe. "What about yours?"

Joe finished tying the laces and, using a bale of hay to support himself, stood up. "They seem like a good fit."

"Mine are comfy too." Will shook his head in surprise. "It's amazing that she happened to choose the right size for each of us."

"Mum must have told Grandma our shoe sizes," Amy said.

Will grinned. "Of course! Now we just need something to skate on."

"Let's have a look at the pond," Sarah said.

The children took off their skates and put their boots back on. Then, leaving the barn, they headed towards the pond, Jock racing ahead as usual.

Surrounded by snow covered trees, the pond looked magical with the sun's rays shining on the ice. While it wasn't enormous, it was still large enough to allow them to skate in circles.

"It's beautiful!" Amy exclaimed.

"Can we skate now?" Sarah asked.

"I'll just test it." Joe gingerly stood on the ice. He waited a few seconds before he walked forward. There was a moment of silence as everyone listened for a noise that would indicate that the ice had cracked, but no sound was heard. He turned to the others. "It seems hard to me."

"It should be," Amy said. "After all, Grandpa said it has been frozen for weeks."

"I know that, but I wanted to make sure," Joe said.

"Can we go ice skating now?" Sarah pleaded. "I haven't been for so long. Please, can we go skating now?"

"Hold on," Joe said. "We've got plenty of time to skate. Let's explore the rest of the property. Look, we haven't even gone up there to see what that building is." He pointed towards the big hill that rose up behind the farmhouse. On top of it was a small, stone hut.

The four children started climbing up the hill. They had roughly reached the halfway mark when Joe grinned at the others. "Let's see who can reach the hut first!"

"Hey! Come back here!" Amy shouted as the two boys raced off. They didn't take the slightest notice of her, so she glanced at her sister. "So, what do you think of the place?"

"Well, it's different from Smugglers Cove," Sarah replied, looking around. "The snow's pretty, but it's tiring walking up this hill in it."

"You're right," Amy agreed. "It's harder than normal, but we're almost there."

When the girls reached the hut, they found the boys lounging on some old wooden chairs. Apart from the chairs, there was an old wooden table.

"Someone must have lived here at one time," Amy said.

"Probably, but a very long time ago," Sarah replied as she ran her finger over the top of the table and noticed how dusty it was.

"Well, since Heather Hills used to be a sheep farm, I would say that one of the farm workers probably slept here," Will said.

Joe looked over at the stone fireplace. "Hey! We could pretend we were camping and light a fire here."

"And toast some crumpets," Sarah piped up, her green eyes gleaming.

"It would be our own private place." Joe looked at the others. "I just thought of something."

"What?" Amy asked.

Why don't we sleep here?" Joe suggested. "We could fix this place up and bring some blankets and books and—"

"Why would we do that?" Sarah interrupted. "We've got nice bedrooms back at the farmhouse."

"Because it would be an adventure!" Joe looked towards Will. "What do you think?"

Will considered Joe's idea. "Well, it would be different. Something we've never done before. And it could be quite fun."

"Exactly," Joe said. "Imagine sitting around a roaring fire playing snap. It would be just us. After all, I don't think we're going to have an adventure while we're staying at Heather Hills, so this would be the closest thing to having one."

"I'm not too keen on the idea," Amy said. "After all, we'd have to bring all of the stuff up to the hut and then, every time we wanted to go to the farmhouse, we'd have to go down the steep hill."

Will grinned. "I didn't know you were against exercise."

"I'm not against exercise," Amy protested. "I just don't know if it's worth it."

"It will be fun," Joe insisted. "And an adventure at the same time. I thought you liked having adventures."

"I do, but I thought we came to Scotland to relax and enjoy ourselves," Amy said.

"Well, if you don't want to come, just Will and I can stay in the hut." Joe looked at his friend. "You'll say yes, won't you?"

Will nodded. "If the girls prefer to laze about, you and I can have an adventure all on our own."

"You wouldn't have an adventure without Sarah and me," Amy said.

"Wouldn't we?" Joe shared a glance with Will. "If the girls weren't with us, we wouldn't have to go slow sometimes."

"We don't slow you down," Amy protested. She looked at Sarah. "Come on, let's show the boys we can do what they can do and sleep in the hut with them."

Sarah hesitated. "Okay. Hey, I wonder if Jock would like to sleep with us. He would keep us nice and warm."

The four children left the hut but, instead of going straight back to the house, they decided to head further up the hill. The top section of the farm bordered a wood and, beyond that, was a mountain that rose steeply into the sky.

Wanting to take a closer look, Joe walked up to the fence. For a few moments he peered into the snowy landscape of trees and bushes before he turned his attention to the mountain. "I wonder why it's called Claw Mountain."

Amy gazed up at the tall mountain. "Probably because the top of it looks like a claw."

Joe nodded. "That's possible, but I don't think so."

"Well, why do you think it's called Claw Mountain then?" Amy questioned, looking at Joe.

"I don't know," Joe admitted. "But it looks exciting and mysterious."

"Exciting? Mysterious?" Sarah shivered. "It looks

creepy to me." She gazed at the snow covered trees. "I wonder if there are any wild animals in these woods."

"There aren't any wild animals here," Will said.

"What do you mean?" Sarah asked. "There are wild animals everywhere."

"Well, what I meant is, I don't think we would come across any animal that would harm us," Will replied. "I expect we would see some wild rabbits, maybe a deer or two, but nothing dangerous."

"How would you know what animals are up here?" Amy asked, curious.

"I studied it in school last year," Will replied.

"If you girls are too scared to explore the mountain, then Will and I can…" Joe paused as Jock suddenly rushed up to the fence and started barking.

"Why is he barking like that?" Sarah asked.

Amy patted Jock and tried to calm him down but it wasn't any use. She turned to the others. "Maybe he smelt something."

Joe scanned the trees. "He probably spotted a rabbit." He suddenly caught sight of a face peering through the branches of a nearby bush.

Will was the first to notice the startled expression on Joe's face. "What's wrong?"

Joe turned around so that he had his back to the woods. He looked at the others. "Don't look now, but there's someone watching us."

CHAPTER 3

A STRANGE CONVERSATION

"What? Where?" Amy exclaimed. Straight away, she looked over Joe's shoulder.

Realizing that the man would have heard Amy's cry, Joe slowly turned around just as a bald headed man emerged.

The man walked up to the fence and thinly smiled at the children. "Did I overhear you talking about Claw Mountain?"

"Yes, we were—" Joe said.

"Jock! Be quiet!" Will interrupted as Jock growled menacingly at the man. The dog barked once more and then stopped.

Joe resumed speaking. "Do you happen to know anything about Claw Mountain? We were thinking of exploring—"

"I wouldn't advise that," the man replied sharply.

Will frowned. "Why not?"

The man looked intently at Will through narrow, pale blue eyes. "It's a dangerous place."

"Why?" Joe asked.

"I wouldn't want you to end up like Harold Rodgers," the man replied.

"Who is he?" Amy asked.

"A hiker who went missing while walking through these woods a month ago," the man said.

Sarah frowned. "Missing?"

"Correct. No one has seen him since. So, if you don't want to end up like Harold Rodgers, don't climb over this fence." The man gazed at the four of them in turn to make sure that they understood the seriousness of what he was saying. He then turned and walked away.

Joe watched him disappear into the woods. "That was strange."

"I'll say," Amy said. "And creepy."

Joe nodded. "It seemed to me as though he was trying to scare us away from Claw Mountain."

"He did a good job of it," Sarah said. "I'm scared."

Amy put an arm around her sister. "Come on, let's forget about the man and explore the farm."

As the two girls and Jock walked away from the fence, Joe looked at Will. "Wasn't it funny the way Jock reacted to him?"

"Yes," Will replied. "We should have asked him what he was doing wandering about in the woods if it was so dangerous. If he was telling the truth about the hiker going missing, then why wasn't he worried?"

"Good point," Joe said. "I wonder what he was doing. Oh, well, I don't suppose we'll see him again."

"I hope not," Will replied. "I didn't like the look of him."

"Neither did I." Joe turned his attention to Claw Mountain. "I wonder how high we could get if we tried climbing it."

"Not far I imagine, it looks pretty steep in some places," Will said. "Hey, we'd better catch up to the girls."

"Let's have a race to see who can reach them first." Joe sprinted off.

Will ran after him and, for the most part, was behind him. He then edged ahead just as they reached the girls. "Yes!" He yelled out as he collapsed onto the snow, exhausted. He waited for a few moments until he had caught his breath before he sat up. As he did so, he saw that Jock, who had been sniffing a bush, suddenly barked and bounded down the snow covered hill. "Where's he going?"

"I don't know." Amy frowned as she caught sight of a man walking his dog on the dirt road below. "Do you think Jock saw the dog?"

"Possibly." Joe waited for a moment until he was sure Jock was heading towards the man, and then he looked at the others. "Let's go and see the man."

As the four hurried down the hill, the two dogs barked at each other. Joe wasn't sure if it was a friendly greeting or an angry one, so he was glad it had stopped by the time they arrived on the scene.

Amy looked at the man with the dog. He was rather old looking with a bushy grey beard, large spectacles, and a thin nose. However, he looked cheerful and nice. He wore a dark green jacket and had a tartan scarf wrapped around his neck.

"Hello," Amy said.

The man smiled at them. "Hello. I've not seen you lot around here before."

"We just came last night," Joe said.

"That explains it then," the man replied. "I've seen the dog before, but not you."

"We're staying with our grandparents," Amy said. She introduced herself and the others.

The man nodded. "My name's McGregor."

"Do you walk along this road often?" Will asked.

Mr McGregor smiled. "Yes, every day. Though, in the wintertime, if it snows really heavily, I stay indoors."

"The two dogs seem to like each other," Sarah said.

Mr McGregor patted the black scottish terrier. "They do indeed. Even though they've only known each other for a short while, they've become the best of friends."

"Have they ever played together? I mean, without the fence between them?" Amy asked.

"Yes, just the other day," Mr McGregor replied.

"Did they enjoy it?" Sarah asked.

The man chuckled. "They liked it so much that I had to literally tear the two of them apart so I could go home for my dinner."

"Do you live nearby?" Joe asked.

The man gazed down the road. "You turn right at that intersection and walk down the road for five or so minutes until you reach another turnoff. You take that road and walk for another ten minutes until you come in sight of a white cottage by the side of the road. That's where I live." He looked at his watch. "I'd best be going now. My wife is cooking some shortbread and I always like to eat it while it's warm."

"Before you go, could I ask you a quick question?" Joe asked.

"Ask away," Mr McGregor said.

Joe pointed to the mountain that rose up behind the farmhouse. "Do you know why that mountain is called Claw Mountain?"

Mr McGregor frowned. "Why do you ask?"

"It seems such a strange name," Joe said. "Is it because the top of it looks like a claw?"

"No," Mr McGregor muttered. He looked down at his dog. "Come Scotty, it's time to go."

"How far up the mountain can you climb?" Joe asked.

Mr McGregor stared at Joe, his grey eyes unflinching. "Stay away from Claw Mountain."

Joe frowned. "Why?"

"Just stay away from it." Mr McGregor pulled on Scotty's lead and quickly walked away.

"That was weird," Amy said. "First that stranger in the woods warned us about Claw Mountain, and now he does."

Joe nodded. "There's something going on."

"Whatever it is, I don't want any part of it," Sarah said. "I came up here to go tobogganing and skating, not to go exploring creepy woods."

"I just feel there's something he wasn't telling us, which is the real reason why he doesn't want us near Claw Mountain," Joe said.

Amy laughed. "You see mysteries everywhere we go. Remember how we went to Wales and you imagined a mystery?"

"Yes, but there was a mystery there!" Joe exclaimed. "My gut feeling was right!"

"Well, yes, you were right that time." Amy gazed up at Claw Mountain. "But I don't see how there could be a mystery here. After all, it's just a mountain. Come on, let's head back to the farmhouse."

Deep in thought, Joe followed the others back to the building. Once inside, they went into the living room to warm themselves by the fire.

Five minutes later, Mr and Mrs Mitchell came into the room. "Enjoying yourselves?"

"Yes, we are," Will said.

"We just explored the property," Amy said. "We—"

"Can we sleep in the hut that's up on the hill?" Joe interrupted. "We saw it while exploring outside."

Mr Mitchell frowned. "Hut? What hut?"

"There's an old hut on top of the hill," Joe explained.

"I think one of the farm workers probably lived in it," Will said.

"It's dusty and dirty, so it hasn't been used for some time, but apart from that, it seems in good condition," Joe said.

"I see." Mr Mitchell looked over at his wife. "What do you say?"

"Before we decide, I think we should have a look inside it to see what condition it's in," Mrs Mitchell said.

"Can you please take a look at it now?" Joe asked.

As Mr Mitchell nodded, the children stood up and, after putting on their boots again, headed outside and up the hill.

Once Mr and Mrs Mitchell had checked that everything was in order and there was no broken glass or anything else that could harm the children, they turned to the four who were standing by the door.

Mr Mitchell shared a glance with his wife. As she nodded, he looked over at Joe. "It looks safe enough, so yes, you can sleep here if you want."

"But mind you, I still want you to come down for breakfast," Mrs Mitchell said.

Joe grinned. "As if I would ever miss breakfast."

Will laughed. "Not even for a mystery?"

"Well, maybe." Joe looked at his father. "Is it okay if we get some wood and light a fire?"

Mr Mitchell nodded. "Just make sure you don't get too close to it or leave anything hanging over the top of it. I wouldn't want to wake up one morning and see that this hut was on fire."

"We'll be careful," Will promised. "I've lit lots of fires

before, so I'll look after it. No fire is going to get out of control while I'm in charge."

"Good to hear," Mr Mitchell said. "Oh, and in case you didn't know, the wood is stored in the barn."

"Yes, we saw it." Amy looked at her mother. "Do you know if Grandma has any old blankets we could use?"

"I'm sure she does." Mrs Mitchell looked at her husband. "We'd better get going." She turned to the children. "Grandpa and Grandma asked us if we wanted to do some shopping in Dunmoore and then go and meet some of their friends. I don't suppose you want to come with us, do you?"

"No, thanks, we'll stay and fix up the hut," Joe said.

"We'd better go and ask Grandma if we can borrow some blankets," Amy said. "Oh, and we'll need a bucket and some rags to clean with."

CHAPTER 4

THE HUT

It was a very happy group of children who made their way into the farmhouse a few minutes later. As the parents got ready to go shopping, the children went to find their grandparents.

While the girls talked to their grandmother about the blankets, Joe found his grandfather and asked him if they could take some of his books up to the hut.

Five minutes later, the children waved goodbye as Mr Mitchell tooted the horn and drove down the driveway.

Once they were out of sight, Joe looked at the girls. "Did Grandma have some blankets we could use?"

Amy nodded. "Did Grandpa say you could take some books?"

"Yes," Joe replied. "As many as we want."

"Let's get started right away then," Sarah said.

"Well, before we carry the blankets and the books up, we'll need to clean the hut," Amy stated.

"Did you ask Grandma where the bucket and rags were?" Joe asked.

Amy frowned. "No, I forgot. We'll just have to search. They shouldn't be that hard to find."

Five minutes later, both a bucket and some rags had been found. With the bucket filled with warm, soapy water, the children trudged up the hill.

Soon, everyone was hard at work making the hut look spic and span. After Joe had finished cleaning the windows, he dropped his rag into the bucket of water and looked at Amy. "How about I go down to the woodpile now? If we're going to have a fire tonight we'll need some wood."

"Okay, you go and get the wood while we finish cleaning," Amy said.

"I'll help you," Will offered. He followed Joe outside and walked down the hill.

It took a number of trips to gather the wood, and it was an exhausted Joe who sat down on one of the wooden chairs fifteen minutes later. "Phew, that was tiring work."

Sarah glanced around the clean cabin. "Now we just need the blankets and books."

"And straw," Amy said.

Sarah frowned. "Why do we need straw?"

"We can put that between the blankets and the floor to make it more comfortable," Amy said.

The children left the hut and walked down the hill to collect the things they needed. Half an hour later, they gazed around in admiration at the clean and cosy looking hut.

The boys had placed the straw under the blankets and the girls had stacked the books from the study in a neat pile.

"This looks so much better." Amy looked at the boys. "What do you think?"

"I must admit it does look better than I expected it would," Joe said.

Sarah collapsed onto the blankets. "It took a while

though."

Joe looked at his watch. "Gosh, it certainly did. Let's do something fun now. The trouble with winter is that there is so much less daylight to do stuff outdoors."

"Yes, that's the bad thing about winter," Sarah agreed. "The days always seem so short."

"At least we've got books to read tonight," Joe said. "Oh, and I need to get that card game from my bedroom."

Will grinned. "The one you always win?"

"Well, yes, but I didn't bring it because of that," Joe protested. "I brought it because it was small and easy to carry. Anyway, enough talking about what we can do later, what shall we do now?"

"We could go ice skating, tobogganing or build snowmen," Will suggested.

"Tobogganing! Let's go tobogganing." Amy looked at the others. "What do you say?"

"Tobogganing," Will said.

"I want to go ice skating," Sarah complained.

"Let's go ice skating first thing tomorrow morning," Joe said.

Sarah grudgingly agreed. "Okay, I suppose we can do that."

Leaving the hut, the children made their way down the hill. But, instead of going directly to the toboggans in the barn, they made a detour to the farmhouse and into the kitchen as they were all feeling hungry.

Ten minutes later, after eating some fruit and biscuits, the children hurried over to the barn. Then, pulling their toboggans behind them, they climbed back up the hill.

Once they had climbed halfway up, Amy made a suggestion. "Let's slide down from here just so we can get used to the toboggans."

Everyone sat down on their toboggans, making sure to dig their feet into the snow to stop them from sliding down.

After checking to see that the others were ready, Amy called out. "Ready, set, go!"

The four children whizzed down the slope, Jock barking as he hurried after them. Being used to the snow, he quickly overtook them.

As the hill was fairly steep, the ride was quite short and, within half a minute, they all came to a stop at roughly the same time.

"That was fun," Sarah said, beaming.

Will looked at Joe. Yes, it was fun, but it was too short. We should go higher next time."

"Yes, let's," Joe said.

So, for the next run, the children climbed twice the distance, which meant that the run down took twice as long. This time, the two boys edged ahead of the girls and came to a stop first.

Will gazed up the hill once more. "Let's go to the highest part. As close as we can get to the fence."

"I'm getting tired," Amy groaned. She sat down on the snow. "I'm not used to trudging up a snow covered hill."

Joe laughed. "And you think we are?"

"Are you saying you're not tired?" Amy said.

"Well, maybe a bit," Joe admitted. "But when was the last time you went tobogganing in Scotland?"

"This is the first time," Amy replied.

"Exactly!" Joe exclaimed. "So let's make the most of it."

"Okay." Amy grabbed her toboggan and started walking up the hill through the thick snow.

Once they had reached the highest point of the property, Joe stopped and sat down. He glanced around as he studied the surroundings—the farmhouse, the barn, the pond, the hut—before turning to the others. "See those two bushes down there? How about the first one to go past those wins?"

Will nodded. "We should be able to make it that far."

"Of course we'll make it that far," Joe said. "We'll go on three. One, two, three!" As soon as he had finished speaking, he released his feet from the snow and placed them on the toboggan. He leaned forward, urging his toboggan to go down the slippery slope.

Once he had done so, he hung on for dear life as the toboggan rushed down the hill, going faster with every passing second.

There were a few bumps along the way and, as he heard Amy yell, he wondered if she had hit one of the bumps. He then heard Sarah cry out and he looked back. Amy and Sarah had both fallen off their toboggans and were getting back on them. As for Will, he was right on his tail.

Joe leaned forward as he attempted to get just that extra amount of speed. A couple of seconds later, Will had edged up beside him. The two boys raced down the hill neck and neck.

Suddenly, Jock appeared beside Joe. Startled, he leaned to the right and his toboggan crashed into Will's.

"Hey!" Will tried to veer to the right, away from Joe, but he couldn't because the toboggans had somehow jammed together.

A moment later, the toboggans hit a rock. The impact sent the boys and their toboggans into the air only to crash down onto the snow moments later. After tumbling down the hill for a few seconds, the boys came to a stop several feet from the bushes.

Joe wiped the snow away from his eyes and caught

sight of the bushes. "I suppose no one wins then."

No sooner were the words out of Joe's mouth when Amy, now back on her toboggan, whipped past. She yelled out in delight. "I won!"

Joe stood up. "I would have won if it hadn't been for Jock."

"You mean I would have won," Will argued.

"Well, who wants a rematch?" Joe looked at Amy who shook her head and then at Will. He also shook his head.

"Why don't we go inside and get a drink?" Amy suggested. "I'm getting thirsty."

~

Ten minutes later, the four children were sitting in the living room by the warm fire. They had just finished drinking mugs of hot cocoa and were feeling relaxed. After a while, everyone's eyes started to close.

As Joe started to doze off, he felt a slobbery tongue on his nose. Opening his eyes, he saw Jock. "Thanks for waking me up boy." He patted the dog. "Now, how about you go and wake up the others?"

Jock barked and jumped off the sofa. With a big grin on his face, Joe watched as the dog went from one child to the other, licking whatever part of the body he could find uncovered.

Once Joe saw that everyone was awake, he stood up. "If we stay here much longer it'll be too late to do anything outside."

Will yawned. "You're right. Come on, let's have a snowball fight."

The two girls followed the boys outside. As soon as the farmhouse door closed behind them, the boys started throwing snowballs at them.

"Hey, not fair!" Amy said, yelling out as she tried to protect her face with her hands. "It's you two against us two."

Joe grinned as he threw another snowball at his sister. "Isn't that fair, two against two?"

"But you're both boys and we're both girls," Amy pointed out. "How is that fair?"

"Well, okay, we'll switch," Joe said. "I'll go with Sarah and you can go with Will."

Amy nodded. "Sounds good."

As the two teams separated, Joe glanced at Sarah. "If we make our way towards the pond and hide in that clump of trees, we can use them as cover. That way, they won't be able to hit us, but we'll be able to hit them."

"Good thinking," Sarah said.

The two children raced towards the pond as the others threw snowballs at them. As soon as Joe and Sarah reached the trees, they stopped. Using the trees as cover, they threw snowballs at Amy and Will.

Joe grinned as he saw the others retreat. "Yes, we've got them on the run!"

Sarah suddenly put her hands out in front of her. "It's snowing!"

Joe glanced around at the snowflakes gently falling. "It will probably stop in a few minutes, so let's wait until then."

The children leaned against the trunk of a big tree and watched the snow fall, knowing that Amy and Will were probably doing the same thing.

Five minutes later, the flakes were falling more quickly and, as Joe looked around, he realized he could no longer see the farmhouse. The snow had dramatically decreased their visibility.

As the snow continued to fall, Joe glanced at Sarah.

"Maybe we should call it quits."

"You mean because of the snow?" Sarah asked.

"Yes," Joe said. "It would be impossible to see Amy or Will. Also, now it's snowing, it's rather chilly."

"Amy! Will!" Sarah called out in a loud voice. There was no reply. She looked around. "Do you suppose they're trying to sneak up behind us?"

Joe looked at the pond. He could see nothing except the snow drifting down and landing on the ice. "Ouch!" He yelled out in surprise as a snowball slammed into his arm. He looked in the direction from which it had come, but all he saw were the snow covered trees. "You were right. One or both of them must have snuck up behind us."

"What do we do? Retreat back to the farmhouse?" Sarah asked.

"No." Determined to get back at whoever had thrown the snowball, Joe made a super large snowball of his own and walked towards the trees.

Once he had reached them, he stopped and listened. It was quiet. Then, a few moments later, he heard a stifled laugh to the left of him. He walked in that direction.

He couldn't see anything or anyone at first and then, for just a few moments, as the snow began to ease up, he caught sight of a figure. Not wanting to miss this golden opportunity, he threw the snowball with all his might.

CHAPTER 5

MIDNIGHT

A moment later, Amy yelled out. Joe smiled in delight, pleased his throw had found its target. He started to walk towards her but, as he caught sight of Will emerging from the trees on the left hand side, he retreated back the way he had come.

By the time he had reached Sarah, the snow had all but stopped and the sun was breaking through the dark clouds.

Joe decided the snowball fight should continue now they could see one another again. "Follow me and we'll surprise them."

Keeping close to the trees, the two stealthily made their way towards their opponents. Soon, they had come up behind Amy and Will who were advancing slowly towards the pond.

Joe eagerly grabbed a handful of snow and flung it at Will. A moment later, snowballs were flying everywhere.

Before long, everyone was exhausted and, after a particularly big snowball hit Joe squarely on his nose, he raised his hands in surrender. "I've had enough." He collapsed onto the snow, worn out.

"Me too," Amy said, collapsing down beside her

brother. She brushed her long brown hair out of her face. "We should do something inside now."

Suddenly, the blast of a horn was heard. Will looked in the direction of the sound and spotted a car heading down the driveway. "They're back."

"Let's go and see if they've got any food," Joe suggested, standing up. He hurried towards the vehicle which had now come to a stop beside the farmhouse.

~

When Sarah glanced out of the window forty minutes later, she was surprised to see that the sun was going down. She quickly shut the book she was reading and turned to the others. "Shouldn't we go and light the fire in the hut so that it will be warm tonight?"

Joe nodded. "Good idea."

Putting on their coats and boots, the children headed up the snowy hill. As the wood had been collected from the barn earlier, there wasn't too much work needed to get the fire going. Ten minutes later, it was burning nicely.

Joe turned to the others. "Anyone feel like a bit of skating before we go back to the house? It's getting close to sunset, but we still have a little bit of time before it gets dark. Or else we could stay in here and play some board games."

"No, let's go outside and go ice skating," Amy said. "We'll have lots of time to play games later."

The four children left the stone hut and, after collecting their skates from the barn, walked over to the pond. Jock followed them but, as he saw that the children were going ice skating, he turned around and walked back to the farmhouse.

None of the children had done much ice skating

before, so they were all a bit unsteady at first. But as five minutes turned into ten minutes and then ten minutes turned into twenty, they grew accustomed to the way the ice felt beneath their feet. It was so much fun going around in circles on the pond that no one seemed to mind when they fell down.

In what seemed like no time at all, Mrs Mitchell walked over to the pond. "It's getting pretty dark. I think you'd better come in now."

Joe didn't really want to come in but, as he looked around, he saw that the sun had set and it was getting rather dark. "Come on, we can go ice skating tomorrow morning."

The children took off their ice skates and followed Mrs Mitchell back into the farmhouse. After tea, they listened as Grandpa and Grandma talked about the times they had spent travelling around Scotland. It wasn't long, however, before the children started to yawn.

"Come on, I think it's about time we went up to the hut," Joe said. "After all, the earlier we get to sleep, the earlier we can get up and go skating again."

The others agreed with him and so, after saying goodnight to the adults, the children left the warm living room and stepped out into the cold night.

Using their torches to light the way, the children, along with Jock, headed up to the stone hut. The fire was burning brightly and the hut felt warm and cosy.

"Why don't we toast some of the crumpets that Grandma gave us?" Amy suggested.

"Oh, yes! Please let's do that," Sarah begged.

It wasn't long before the hut was filled with the delicious smell of toasted crumpets. Having completely woken up after the walk to the hut and the food, the children decided to play a few games of snap before going to bed.

Afterwards, Joe picked up another log and placed it onto the fire. "That should keep it going until morning."

The children put on their pyjamas and climbed under the blankets. Jock nestled between the two girls and, before long, everyone was sound asleep.

A couple of hours later, Sarah suddenly awoke. As she sat up, she felt cold. Seeing that the fire was quite low, she decided to put another log on it. She had just snuggled back under the blankets when she heard a noise.

At first she ignored it, but then curiosity got the better of her. Throwing back the blankets, she walked to the door and pulled it slightly ajar. The noise sounded like a motor, but what sort of a motor?

Gathering up her courage, she stepped outside. She shone her torch around, seeing if there was any movement. There wasn't.

Hearing the noise again, she looked upwards. The noise seemed to be coming from up above. Listening, she realized that it was the noise of a plane engine. But where was it? She couldn't see a light but, for that matter, she couldn't see the moon. Maybe the clouds were covering it.

As a gust of wind blew in the direction of the hut, she shivered. It was too cold to stay outside any longer. She turned and hurried back into the hut. Soon, all thoughts of the mysterious plane were far from her mind as she drifted off to sleep.

~

The children were eating breakfast the next morning when Sarah suddenly remembered what she had heard the previous night. Swallowing a mouthful of porridge, she looked at the others. "I heard a plane last night."

Joe frowned. "A plane? When?"

"I'm not sure what time it was, but the fire had burnt down quite low, so it was probably sometime after midnight," Sarah said.

Joe listened intently as his sister quickly explained what had happened the previous night. Once she had finished speaking, he frowned. "Why would a plane be flying around here in the middle of the night?"

"I don't know," Sarah said. "It was very strange. I meant to tell you when I woke up, but I forgot."

"Are you sure it was a plane?" Amy asked.

Sarah nodded. "Yes, I'm sure."

"What's this I hear you talking about?" Mr Mitchell asked as he walked into the kitchen and opened the fridge.

"I heard a plane last night," Sarah said.

Mr Mitchell frowned as he poured himself a drink of milk. "So?

"Well, I thought it was unusual," Sarah said.

"Planes fly at all times of the day," Mr Mitchell said.

"So you don't think there was anything strange about the plane?" Joe questioned.

Mr Mitchell shook his head as he washed his glass. "Just because it was flying at night doesn't mean it's strange. Planes often flew over our house in Danfield during the night."

"But this isn't the city, it's the country," Joe said.

"Well, yes, but there must be some planes that fly at night in the country," Mr Mitchell replied.

"I suppose so," Joe said.

~

After breakfast, the children decided to go ice skating again. They were all enjoying themselves immensely when Mrs Mitchell walked across the snow. She smiled at the four as they skated around in a circle. "Are you having fun?"

Joe nodded. "Come and skate with us!"

Mrs Mitchell shook her head. "No, I had my fair share of ice skating when I was younger."

"Why don't you do it now?" Sarah said. "Come on, it will be fun!"

Mrs Mitchell shook her head. "No, I'm happy to leave it to you children. Oh, I just came to tell you that Grandpa and Grandma have invited us to go out for a drive with them. So we'll be out for a few hours but back in time for lunch."

As Mrs Mitchell left, Jock bounded out of the farmhouse and ran across to the children. As he reached the pond, he stopped.

Joe, who was at the far end of the pond, smiled as he saw the dog advance towards the ice. "I think Jock's going to join us."

The others stopped skating and gazed in amusement as the dog put a paw onto the slippery surface. Then he tentatively put all four paws on the ice. As he attempted to move across the pond towards them, the children couldn't help laughing. It was so funny to see him trying to cross the ice.

As Jock slid around and around, unable to control which way he was going, he barked in puzzlement. After glancing at the children, he turned around and tried to get off the ice. But he couldn't. He just kept on sliding this way and that.

Joe looked at Will. "Come on, let's help Jock off the

ice."

The two skated towards the dog and gave him a helping hand. With a joyful bark, he bounded away and headed back to the farmhouse.

CHAPTER 6

JOCK DISAPPEARS

Five minutes later, the adults climbed into the car and, with a toot and a wave, drove down the driveway. The children continued skating on the pond for another half hour or so before, tired out, they decided to head inside.

Even though they had eaten breakfast just a few hours earlier, all the skating seemed to have made them extra hungry. They found some biscuits and some lemonade in the kitchen and sat down. Once they had rested for a while, they decided to build a snowman.

Making their way outside again, Amy decided to build a snowman with Sarah, while Joe joined forces with Will. More than half an hour had passed before both teams declared that they had finished. Deciding to leave the snowmen for the adults to judge the winner, they headed back inside.

As they made their way into the living room and clustered around the fire to warm themselves, Amy suddenly frowned. She glanced around anxiously.

Joe was the first to notice the concerned look on Amy's face. "What's wrong?"

"I was just thinking about Jock," Amy said.

"What about him?" Will muttered, sitting down on one of the chairs that was closest to the fireplace.

"I haven't seen him for ages. I wonder where he is," Amy replied. "I think I'll go and look for him." She went to the front door and called his name loudly, but he didn't appear.

"He's probably chewing on his bone somewhere," Joe said.

"Maybe." Amy sat down and twirled a strand of brown hair around her finger as she thought about Jock. When the grandfather clock chimed a quarter of an hour later, she stood up. "Something's wrong. Jock wouldn't stay away all this time. I'm going to see if I can find him."

"What if he's snoozing away in one of the bedrooms?" Sarah said. "I remember he ran back to the house after Joe and Will helped him off the ice. Grandma or Grandpa may have let him inside."

"I'll have a look," Amy said.

As Sarah hurried after her sister, Joe looked at Will. "What do you think?"

"I think they'll find Jock sleeping in one of the bedrooms," Will said.

"So you don't think we should help them search?" Joe asked.

"Why bother?" Will questioned.

"Well, you stay here and I'll help them look." Joe raced after the girls.

The search didn't take long and, within five minutes, the three were back in the living room.

"Did you find him?" Will asked.

Amy shook her head despondently. "No. And I'm worried. It isn't like Jock to disappear like this."

"Did you check his kennel?" Will asked.

"Yes, and he's not there either," Sarah replied.

Seeing how worried the girls looked, Joe decided to relieve some of the tension. "Come on, let's go outside and have another toboggan race."

"No, I want to search for Jock," Amy said.

"But we've just searched the house," Joe replied. "What else do you suggest we do?"

"Perhaps we could follow his paw prints," Sarah suggested.

"Yes, that's a good idea," Amy replied. "After all, it snowed early this morning so there shouldn't be many prints out there."

The children headed outside. It didn't take them long to spot some paw prints. They went up the hill and to the stone hut. The prints then meandered around for a while before continuing upwards to the fence.

Joe came to a stop as he saw that the prints disappeared through a hole in the wire. "I didn't see that hole when we explored earlier."

Will shook his head. "No, but that's probably because we didn't come this far. Remember how Jock saw that man down by the road and tore down the hill? Well, I think that happened before we reached this point."

"You could be right," Joe replied.

"I wonder who or what made the hole in the fence," Sarah said.

"Whoever the culprit was, it seems recent," Will stated as he knelt down and examined the fence in detail.

"So what do we do now?" Joe asked.

"Isn't it obvious? We go through the hole," Amy said.

Maybe Jock went to the woods and hurt himself. Maybe he got attacked by some wild animals," Sarah said.

"There aren't any wild animals out here," Joe replied.

"Besides, if there were some wild animals, wouldn't someone have reported it to the local constable?"

"Maybe they have," Amy said. "After all, we haven't spoken to the police so we don't—"

"Why don't we go through and have a look?" Sarah interrupted. "The only way we'll know for sure where Jock is, is if we find him. And we're not going to do that if we argue amongst ourselves."

"I'm not arguing," Joe protested.

Amy glanced at her watch. "Mum and Dad should be back soon, so if we're going to search for Jock before they get back we need to hurry."

"Okay, we'll have a look." Joe knelt down next to the hole and crawled through it. Once he was through the small gap, he waited for the others to join him.

Amy led the way as they walked in the direction of Claw Mountain. As she walked through the trees, she called out. "Jock!"

There was no reply. The children studied the ground as they walked along, looking for any sign of paw prints. However, as the snow was disturbed in numerous places, probably due to the woodland creatures, they weren't able to see any.

The children had been searching for ten minutes when Sarah suddenly stopped. She looked at the others excitedly. "Did you hear that? I think it was Jock."

Everyone fell silent for the next minute as they listened. Apart from some birds chirping, no other sound could be heard. There wasn't even a gust of wind to rustle the tree branches.

Suddenly, barking broke though the silence.

"It's Jock!" Amy exclaimed. The others quickly followed her as she dodged between numerous trees and bushes as she headed in the direction of the sound. A few minutes later, the trees and bushes parted to reveal an entrance to a disused mine. Just then, the barking stopped.

Joe walked forward and gazed around with interest. "This looks as though it's been closed for a while."

"I wonder where poor Jock is." Sarah called out loudly. "Jock!"

Suddenly, barking erupted from inside the mine. Amy hurried to where the mine entrance had been boarded up and put her ear up against a plank. "Yes! It's him. He must be trapped inside." She called to Jock. "Don't worry boy. We'll get you out soon."

Sarah frowned. "How did he get in there?"

"Maybe through here," Joe suggested, walking over to where there were a couple of broken planks on the far right hand side of the mine entrance.

Eager to get to Jock first, Amy rushed over and attempted to squeeze though the hole. But she couldn't even make it a quarter of the way through as the space was too small. Disappointed, she wriggled out and stood up. "It's not big enough for me."

"I could try," Sarah suggested. "I might be small enough."

The others watched as Sarah knelt down and attempted to succeed where her sister had failed just a few moments earlier. But, even though she was smaller than Amy, she was still too big.

As Sarah crawled back out of the hole, Joe looked at Will. "I say we try to pull off one of the planks."

Will nodded. "That could work, but we don't have any tools to remove a plank."

"Maybe we won't need any." Amy pointed to a plank to the left of the hole. "That one looks as though it could come away from the rest with a good yank or two."

"Let's see if you're right," Joe said. "Come on Will, give me a hand."

While the girls watched, the boys took hold of the plank and pulled with all their might. Nothing happened for a few moments and then, suddenly, with a really loud creak, it came away, causing the boys to fall down in the snow.

"Phew!" Joe said. "For a moment, I wasn't sure if we were going to get it off."

Will studied the gap that was now a bit larger. "I wonder if we'll need to remove another plank."

"We shouldn't need to, especially if we crawl. I'll go first." Amy knelt down and started crawling on her knees. Once she was halfway through, she yelled out. "It's large enough for me!"

"I'll go next," Will said.

After Will went through without any trouble, Sarah followed him. It was then Joe's turn. Once he was through, he realized how dark it was. The only light came from the gaps between the planks and the small opening through which they had just entered.

"We should have brought a torch," Joe said.

Going as fast as they could in the dim light, the children hurried over to where a hole in the ground was visible.

CHAPTER 7

VOICES

As soon as Amy saw Jock, she cried out. "There he is!"

As the dog saw the children, he wagged his tail joyfully.

Sarah knelt down and studied the hole that was about five feet deep. "I wonder how he got in there."

"He was probably chasing something," Will said.

"Maybe an animal raced through that hole in the mine entrance and Jock followed him," Amy suggested. "Now, let's see if we can get him out."

Joe glanced around. "With what? I don't see anything."

"We must do something." Amy gazed down at Jock who was trying his hardest to climb out of the hole. "I wonder if someone could climb down there and lift him out."

"I don't know," Joe admitted. "The hole looks a bit too deep for that."

"I'll try," Will offered. "After all, I'm probably the strongest." He grinned at Joe who playfully punched him.

"Okay, you see what you can do," Joe said.

Will sat down and eased himself down into the hole. As his feet touched the bottom, he realised how deep the hole actually was. It hadn't looked so deep earlier but, now that he was standing in it, he realised it was face high. "Okay, here goes nothing."

The others watched on as Will bent down and attempted to lift Jock up. But the animal was much heavier than he had imagined and he could barely lift him off the ground let alone hand him up to the others. He shook his head. "It's no use. I can't even get him close to the top of the hole."

"You could try again," Amy suggested.

"No, he's too heavy," Will said. "Help me up, please."

Joe and Amy gave Will a helping hand and, a moment or two later, all four children were gazing down at Jock.

"So what do we do now?" Sarah asked, despondently.

"I think we'd better go and get a rope so we can pull him up," Will suggested.

"But then we'd have to go back to the farmhouse. Isn't there something we can do here? Maybe there's something in the mine that we can use." Amy glanced around. As she did so, she suddenly got an idea. "Hey, you know the plank you pulled off? What if we were to use that?"

"Are you suggesting we lean the plank up against the side of the hole?" Joe asked.

"Exactly," Amy said, smiling. "Do you think it will work?"

"Well, we won't know if we don't try it," Joe replied.

"I'll get the plank." Will walked back to the hole and crawled out. Half a minute later, he was pushing the plank through the hole.

Joe took hold of it. "Let's see if it's going to be long enough." He placed it into the hole, leaning it up against the walls as much as possible. Fortunately, it was just the right length.

With a joyful bark, Jock raced up the plank and into the arms of Amy. She hugged him and planted a kiss on his head. "I'm so glad you're safe."

"Let's get out of here before we lose Jock again," Sarah suggested.

Joe glanced around the mine. "I would like to explore more, but I can't do it without a torch, so we may as well go."

Jock was the first out of the mine followed by Sarah, then Will and Joe. As Joe looked behind him, he realised Amy hadn't appeared. He called out. "What are you doing?"

There was no answer, so Joe crawled back through the hole. Looking around, he saw that Amy hadn't moved at all. She was still standing next to the hole that Jock had been trapped in. "What are—"

"Quiet!" Amy whispered.

Joe walked over to his sister. "What is it?"

"I heard voices," Amy said.

Joe looked at her in disbelief. "What? Here?"

Amy nodded. "Yes, but they've stopped now."

"What exactly did you hear?" Joe asked, following his sister as she walked back to the entrance of the mine.

"I'll tell you in a minute," Amy said, crawling out through the hole.

Will looked at the two of them. "What took you so long?"

"Well, just as I was about to follow you, I thought I heard something," Amy explained. "I wasn't sure what it was, so I waited. A few seconds later, I heard people talking."

"People talking? In the mine?" Will questioned.

Joe frowned. "Are you sure you weren't imagining things?"

"Quite sure," Amy stated.

"Are you sure you weren't hearing our voices or someone else's outside the mine?" Joe asked.

"I'm sure," Amy replied.

"But what would people be doing down there when it's closed?" Will asked. "It doesn't make any sense."

"No, it doesn't," Joe agreed.

"Let's see if we can hear them now," Will said, determined to get to the bottom of this mystery. He walked back to the hole and crawled through.

Joe and Amy followed him. They were soon standing on the exact spot where Amy had stood just moments ago. They fell silent, their ears alert for any sound.

After listening for a minute, Amy shook her head. "I can't hear anything now."

"Me neither," Will said.

"Neither can I." Joe looked at Amy. "Maybe it was an animal you heard."

Amy shook her head. "No, I heard people talking." She walked back to the hole. "At least I think I did."

"Did you hear anything?" Sarah asked, glancing towards the three as she patted Jock.

Joe shook his head. "I'm inclined to think that Amy's ears must have been playing tricks on her."

"Then what about Sarah when she heard the plane last night?" Amy asked.

"What about it?" Joe said.

"Well, couldn't the plane and the voices be connected?" Amy said.

Joe hesitated. "I suppose so, but we don't have any proof that there was a plane. And we don't have any proof that there was someone in the mine. Anyway, let's walk and talk at the same time."

The children left the mine and walked back through the woods to the hole in the fence. They squeezed through it and trooped down the hill to the stone hut.

As they did so, Amy looked at Joe. "Why don't you believe Sarah and me?"

"What do you mean?" Joe asked.

"I thought you were always up for a mystery, but then when one comes your way you back away," Amy replied.

"I'm always up for a mystery, but one hasn't come my way," Joe said. "Just because you heard something and Sarah heard something doesn't mean there's a mystery. After all, how could those two be connected?"

"I don't know," Amy admitted.

"Hey, they're back!" Will shouted as a car drove down the driveway.

Jock barked and tore down the hill, quickly followed by the children. After exchanging greetings, the children showed the adults the two snowmen they had built earlier.

Mr Mitchell admired the snowmen. "You've done a fine job with these."

"Which one is better? This one or that one?" Sarah asked, pointing to each one in turn.

"I'm not sure." Mr Mitchell looked at his father. "What do you think?"

Grandpa smiled. "They're both winners in my eyes."

"You're just saying that because you don't want to hurt our feelings," Amy said.

"No, he's not. They truly are winners." Grandma smiled. "Now, are any of you hungry? I thought I'd go and bake some scones."

"I'm hungry!" Amy said.

Joe grinned. "Me too!"

"And me!" Sarah piped up.

Grandma looked at her watch. "It will take me twenty minutes to make them."

"Okay, we'll play until then." As the adults retreated to the warmth of the farmhouse, Joe looked at the others. "What shall we do?"

"Well, what is there to do?" Amy said. "We've explored all around the farm, gone ice skating, tobogganing, seen the mine—"

"Of course!" Joe interrupted. "I was going to ask Grandpa about Claw Mountain."

With Joe leading the way, the children searched for him. They found him in the study examining a very old book. As the children entered the room, he took off his spectacles and smiled at them. "Are you tired of playing in the snow?"

"No," Will said. "But Joe wanted to ask you about Claw Mountain."

"What do you want to know?" Grandpa said. "It's just a mountain."

"What about the name?" Joe said. "I spoke to Mr McGregor about the mountain but he seemed as though he was hiding something."

"Hiding something? What do you mean?" Grandpa asked.

"Well, when I asked why it was called Claw Mountain, he said he had to go," Joe replied.

"Well, maybe he had something to do," Grandpa said. "What's with all the questions? Does it really matter why it's called Claw Mountain?"

Joe shook his head. "No, I was just interested." Seeing he wasn't going to get anything else out of his grandfather, he thanked him for his help and turned to the others. "Let's play a game in the living room for a while."

"Good idea," Sarah said.

After they had played a couple of games of snap, Grandma came into the room and announced that the scones were ready.

A minute later, after everyone was seated at the table, the hot scones were taken out of the oven and set down on the table.

Will was the first to grab a scone. A moment later, he grinned. "These are absolutely scrumptious."

"That's good to hear." Grandma smiled. "I hope all of you enjoy them."

Joe laughed. "You can be sure I will."

After the scones were eaten, the children lazed around by the fire. An hour or so later, Joe glanced out of the window and saw it was almost sunset. "It's going to be dark soon. If we're going to do anything outside, we'd better do it now."

"We could play a board game," Sarah suggested, somewhat reluctant to leave the cosy warmth of the fire.

"Why don't we go tobogganing first?" Joe said. "There'll be plenty of time to play board games when it gets dark. We should do something outside while we still have the light."

As Amy and Sarah were happy to stay indoors for a while longer, the boys grabbed their toboggans and headed up the hill.

CHAPTER 8

THE CREATURE

Joe stopped as he reached the stone hut. "I think this will be far enough."

Will sat down on his toboggan. "Okay. Ready, set, go!"

Down the hill they went. This time, they went even faster than the previous day due to the compacted snow. They zigzagged crazily over the bumps, reaching the barn at roughly the same time.

"We were even that time." Joe grinned as he caught sight of Amy and Sarah walking towards them. "Well, well. Look who's coming to join us."

"I thought you were going to stay inside," Will said.

"Well, it got a bit boring reading, so we thought we'd join you," Amy said.

The boys waited for the girls to grab their toboggans from the barn and then, all together, they plodded up the hill.

For the next ten minutes, the children raced each other down the slope, but all too soon the light began to fade. Before they went inside, they walked up to the stone hut and got the fire going. Then, satisfied that it would be warm inside the hut when they were ready to go to bed, they ran down the hill and into the farmhouse.

~

The next morning, as everyone awoke, Joe glanced around at the others. "Did anyone hear a plane last night?"

"No, I was sound asleep for the entire night," Will said.

Amy yawned. "Me too. I meant to wake up and check, but as soon as my head touched the pillow, I was asleep."

Joe looked across at Sarah. "How about you?"

"I woke up once," Sarah said. "I listened, but didn't hear anything, so I went back to sleep."

"Well, I woke around half past three and I didn't hear anything either." Joe frowned. "I wish I knew why that plane flew over the farm, but I suppose I'll never know."

"Let's think about what we're going to do today instead," Amy suggested.

"Well, we could walk down the road to Dunmoore," Joe replied. "Dad said something about a lake this side of the village, so we could take a look at it. If it was frozen like the pond, we could skate on it."

"Good idea," Amy said. "The pond has been fun but, since a lake would be bigger, that would be even more fun."

A few minutes later, the children were racing down the hill to the farmhouse. As soon as they were in the kitchen, Amy went up to her father. "Do you think the lake in the village will be frozen?"

"I imagine it will be," Mr Mitchell said. "It was very cold last night. I know that because I accidentally left the window open. It was so cold I woke up. Oh, that reminds me." He turned to Joe. "Just as I was about to close the window, a plane flew overhead. Weren't you saying something about hearing a plane the other night?"

Sarah nodded. "That was me."

"Did you see it or just hear it?" Will asked.

"Well, there was a full moon, so I managed to get a glimpse of it as it passed overhead. It looked and sounded like a small plane to me," Mr Mitchell said. "However, I could be mistaken."

"What direction was it flying in?" Joe asked.

"North. Straight over Claw Mountain." Mr Mitchell smiled. "What's with the twenty questions? Another mystery?"

Joe laughed. "I wish."

Mr Mitchell stood up and tousled his son's brown hair. "You're always thinking about mysteries, aren't you?"

Amy laughed. "That and food!"

Joe grinned back. "They're two of the best things in life. Food and mysteries." As Mr Mitchell left the room, the boy looked at Sarah. "Do you think the plane you heard was heading towards Claw Mountain?"

"Maybe. I really don't know," Sarah admitted. "As I couldn't see it, I can't say for sure, but the noise did seem to come from somewhere near Claw Mountain."

"I see," Joe said. "Well, the first thing we need to do is find out where the nearest airport is."

Suddenly, an anguished cry rang out. Amy's face froze in fear. "Who was that?"

All four children shot to their feet and hurried out of the room. They stopped hurriedly as they saw a figure at the bottom of the stairs. It was Grandma. She appeared to be in a lot of pain and was clutching her leg.

~

Fifteen minutes later, the children waved goodbye as Mr Mitchell's car disappeared down the driveway.

"I do hope Grandma's going to be okay," Sarah said anxiously.

Amy hugged her sister. "I'm sure she will be. After all, Grandpa didn't think her leg was too badly hurt, but he thought it best to get it looked at by a doctor."

"I wonder when they'll be back," Will said.

"Not for a while," Joe replied. "Didn't Grandpa say it was quite a distance to the hospital?"

"I think so," Amy said. "So, shall we see what the shops are like in Dunmoore?"

"We can go skating as well," Will said.

"Well, we should have a look at the lake first. If the ice is hard enough, we can always go back with our skates," Amy replied.

Joe's face lit up. "Hey! Didn't Dad say something about Dunmoore having a bakery?"

"But we just ate," Sarah said. "Surely you can't be hungry already."

"No, but my tummy's always got space for a cream bun," Joe replied with a twinkle in his eye. "Besides, I'd like to ask someone about the mine we saw so we could do the two things at the same time."

"Okay. Let's go now and take Jock with us. I'm sure he'd like a walk." Will called out. "Jock!" A few moments later, the animal barked and tore around the corner of the barn.

Amy smiled at the brown dog as she patted him. "Would you like to go for a walk Jock?"

The dog wagged his tail furiously in reply. Sarah joined her sister in patting Jock and he gave her a big slobbery lick on her face. She wrapped her arms around him. "You're such a darling dog."

~

It was a fifteen minute walk to the small village, but the children enjoyed every minute of it as they gazed in delight at the snow covered fields.

Before they reached the village, they saw the lake. Straight away, they realised it was frozen because a dozen or so people were skating on it.

"It's bigger than I expected," Will said. "Shall we come back here this afternoon?"

"Yes, it would be fun to skate on it." Joe resumed walking. "But let's see what the village is like."

As they came upon Dunmoore five minutes later, they saw it was far smaller than Smugglers Cove. There was a bakery, a general store, a church, a police station and two other little shops.

The children headed to the bakery which, according to the sign, was called Penny Olive Bakery. A jolly faced woman with short red hair greeted the children as they gazed in awe at the assortment of cakes, buns and scones. "Hello. I haven't seen you lot around here before."

Amy smiled at the woman. "We're staying with our grandparents up at Heather Hills."

Mrs Olive nodded. "Ah, yes, Mr and Mrs Mitchell. So, how's life treating them?"

"Not so good." Joe quickly explained what had happened that morning to his grandmother.

The woman frowned. "Oh dear. I hope she's going to be alright. I always thought that the staircase was too steep."

"Oh, so you know the house do you?" Will said, surprised.

Mrs Olive nodded. "Yes. A nice old chap lived there some time ago. He used to be a sheep farmer but in the end his sheep became like family to him and he couldn't bear to sell them. He'd put them in the barn at night to keep them warm and he kept them until they died of old age."

"What about the man? What happened to him?" Amy asked.

"Well, shortly after all the sheep died, he got attacked by the creature so he left Dunmoore," Mrs Olive replied.

Will frowned. "The creature?"

"What are you talking about?" Joe asked.

Mrs Olive hesitated. "Have you not heard about the creature that roamed these parts?"

"No, we haven't," Amy replied.

"What happened?" Joe asked, eagerly.

"Well, about a year and a half ago, a creature was sighted near the gold mine at the base of Claw Mountain," Mrs Olive explained. "Over the next few months, quite a number of workers were attacked by the creature and eventually the mining company was forced to close the mine because the workers refused to work there."

"What sort of creature was it?" Will asked.

"Some kind of large cat," the woman replied. "At least, that's what the people who were attacked thought it was. But, as most of the attacks occurred at night, there were varying accounts of the exact size and colour of the creature. Though, the one thing that remained the same in all the descriptions was that it was a large animal with sharp claws."

"Is that why it's called Claw Mountain?" Joe asked. "Because of the claws that the creature had?"

"Yes," Mrs Olive said. "The people who were injured

were found with big claw marks on their bodies and, after a number of attacks, rumours started to spread about these claw marks and how the creature lived on this mountain, so then it became known as Claw Mountain. Anyway, after the mine closed, one of the miners decided to see if he could find the creature's hideout."

"What was his name?" Joe asked.

"I forget, but he had a long scar on one side of his face," Mrs Olive said. "Resenting the fact that the animal had cost him his job, he borrowed a rifle and hiked into the woods." The woman glanced around the bakery. "I was serving customers in this store six months ago when the postman burst through the door. He told me that the man had just limped into the police station. Apparently, he had found the creature near the river and shot the animal, injuring his leg in the process. Several of the village folk, myself included, went into the woods to see the body, but when we got there, all we saw was a pool of blood."

"Golly," Sarah said. "I wonder what happened to the animal."

Mrs Olive sighed. "I don't know. We never found it. The mine worker said that the creature must have had enough strength to return to his hideout. We followed the trail of blood but, since it led to the river, there was no way of knowing what had happened to the animal. However, the miner, confident that the animal was dead, pleaded with the mine operators to open the mine again so he could get his job back. But the owners said that they would need to wait six months before they did that to make certain that the animal was dead."

"Oh, so the mine should be opening soon," Sarah said.

"Yes, in January so…" Mrs Olive paused as the bell on the door suddenly tinkled and a customer walked in. "Excuse me for a moment."

As the woman walked away, Amy glanced at the others. "I wonder if that's why the man in the woods told us not to explore Claw Mountain. He probably didn't want us to meet the creature."

Joe shook his head. "You heard what Mrs Olive just said. The animal hasn't been seen since the man shot it."

"Let's ask her about the hiker who went missing when she comes back," Will said.

"Good idea." As Joe's stomach rumbled, he grinned. "Let's decide what we're going to order while we're waiting."

CHAPTER 9

THE MINE

By the time Mrs Olive had finished serving her customer, the children had decided to buy some jam tarts and some cream buns. Choosing a table that was near the window, they sat down.

Amy took a bite of one of the jam tarts. "These are delicious."

"Thank you," Mrs Olive said. "They were made just this morning."

As Joe finished eating the portion of the tart that was in his mouth, he smiled. "And they taste like it. Oh, if you don't mind, I have another question."

"Ask anything you like," Mrs Olive said.

"Have you heard of a man called Harold Rodgers?" Joe asked.

The woman frowned. "Harold Rodgers? That name sounds familiar, but I can't think why."

"Someone told us he went missing a month ago while hiking in the woods," Will said.

Mrs Olive nodded. "Ah, yes. Now I remember. He was a youngish man with spiked hair. He came in here one afternoon and told me he was going on a weekend hike around Claw Mountain to see if he could see any sign of the creature. However, I got the impression he wasn't telling the truth."

"What do you mean?" Amy asked.

The woman frowned. "I don't know what it was, but there was something strange about him. The way he smiled at me. And the way he talked loudly about finding the animal, almost as though he wanted everyone to hear what he was saying. After he left, I talked to the postman and the local constable and I discovered that he had told them exactly what he had told me. No one has seen him since."

"Has anyone else gone missing lately?" Will questioned.

"Not that I know of." Mrs Olive looked at the children. "Now, is that all the questions you have?"

"I have one more," Joe said. "Is it usual for planes to fly over Dunmoore at night?"

"I'm not sure," the woman replied. "I'm a heavy sleeper, so I haven't noticed any. Why?"

"Well, for the past two nights, a plane has flown over Heather Hills," Joe said.

"Hmm, that does seem unusual," Mrs Olive said.

"Where's the nearest airport?" Will asked.

Mrs Olive thought for a moment. "As far as I know, there's only one airport nearby, and that's at Lochnell."

"Is that north of here?" Joe asked.

Mrs Olive shook her head. "No, why?"

"My father saw a plane last night, and he said that it was heading north, straight over Claw Mountain," Joe replied.

The woman frowned. "That's strange. There's nothing in that direction except mountains."

"What about another airport, somewhere further away?" Amy asked.

Mrs Olive shook her head. "No. The mountain range extends north for quite a long way. There used to be a few farms to the left and right of the woods, but they've been deserted ever since the mine closed down."

"Okay, thanks." As the woman walked away, Joe looked at the others. "So, what do you make of that?"

"That the plane wasn't heading to Lochnell," Will replied.

"Correct," Joe said. "And, if it wasn't heading there, then where was it heading?"

"What about those farms that the woman mentioned?" Sarah said.

"I did think of that," Joe admitted, "but where would the plane land?"

"In a field," Sarah replied.

"Well, I shouldn't think there would be many fields flat enough for a plane to land in that area," Joe said. "Anyway, I don't think we're going to get an answer just sitting here, so let's take a walk around the village. Maybe the exercise will get our brains working."

As soon as the tarts and buns had been eaten up, the children said goodbye to Mrs Olive and walked down the main street.

~

After spending the next ten minutes exploring the small village, Joe turned to the others. "Let's go back to the farmhouse now."

"And do what?" Amy questioned.

"I want to explore the mine," Joe replied. "But we'll need a torch, so that's why we need to go to the farmhouse."

"But what about the creature?" Sarah asked.

Joe laughed. "If we had been here a year ago, I wouldn't have wanted to explore the mine. But I'm sure the animal's dead now so we don't have anything to fear."

"What about the man who went missing a month ago?" Amy questioned. "What if he was attacked by the creature?"

"But you heard what Mrs Olive told us," Joe replied. "No one has seen the creature for the past six months, so isn't it reasonable to assume that—"

"But what about the man in the woods?" Amy interrupted. "And what about the man we met walking his dog? If they told us to stay away from Claw Mountain, we should do as they say."

"If you want to stay behind you can, but I'm going exploring." Joe looked at Will. "Are you coming with me?"

Will looked at the girls. "Come on, let's all go. It's not as much fun if it's just us two."

Amy sighed. "Oh, alright, we should probably stick together." She looked at her sister. "What do you say?"

"I'll come, but only if we can go skating afterwards," Sarah replied.

Joe grinned. "Deal."

~

Since the children didn't think it would be a good idea for Jock to go with them, he was tied up next to his kennel and given some dog biscuits to keep him happy.

Once Joe and Will had grabbed their torches, they climbed up the hill. After crawling through the hole in the fence, they walked through the woods.

As they reached the mine, Joe looked around. It looked exactly the same as it had the last time they had seen it. He contemplated searching for another entrance as he felt sure there was one, but since he was eager to explore the mine, he decided the search could always be done later. He switched on his torch and crawled through the hole. The girls followed with Will bringing up the rear.

As soon as Joe swung his torch around, he realised that they would be here for a while. The cave they were in was quite big and there were four tunnels leading out of it in different directions.

"Let's explore the tunnel closest to us first." Joe led the way down the tunnel. At first, the girls had fun exploring the tunnels but, after they had walked down three of them and found nothing of interest, they were ready to leave the mine.

However, the boys didn't want to, so the girls reluctantly agreed to go down the last tunnel. They had just started walking down it when, rounding a bend, Joe saw something that caught his eye. "Look at this!"

As everyone crowded around the hole that had been dug in the widest part of the tunnel, Joe shone his torch down it and saw it was at least fifteen feet to the bottom. "Gosh, that's a big hole."

"I wonder how strong this ladder is," Will said, looking at the wooden ladder which descended into the hole.

Joe switched off his torch and put it into his pocket. "Well, there's only one way to find out."

"You're not thinking of going down there, are you?" Amy asked, shocked.

"Why not?" Joe said as he took hold of the top part of the ladder and prepared to step down into the hole.

"Anything could be down there," Amy replied. "And if that ladder has been there for ages, I'm sure that some of the wood has rotted away."

"I'll be careful," Joe said. "I promise." The others watched on as he went down the ladder. There were a few anxious moments as he stopped from time to time, but then he reached the ground below. He switched on his torch. "Come down!"

"Why? What's the point?" Amy yelled.

"What's down there?" Will shouted. He gazed down at Joe, only to see him disappear from view a moment later.

The others waited for him to reappear, but he didn't. Just when they were wondering if something had happened to him, he reappeared.

"Where were you?" Amy exclaimed. Joe didn't answer, but climbed up the ladder. As he reached the top, she saw a gleam in his eyes and realised something was up. "What did you see down there?"

Joe looked at his sister. "You were right."

"Right about what?" Amy asked.

"About hearing voices, because I just heard them myself," Joe replied.

CHAPTER 10

UNDERGROUND

Will gasped. "What?"

"I didn't hear much," Joe admitted, "but enough to know that there were two men down there. And, if I were to take a guess, I would say they are not the only ones."

"But why?" Sarah shuddered. "I can't think of any reason why people would be in this dark place."

Joe looked down the hole. "The only way we'll know for sure is if we go down and listen to their conversation."

"But what if they see us?" Amy protested.

"If you're worried, you can stay up there, but I'm not," Joe replied. "And I'm sure Will isn't either. After all, this could be the start of another mystery."

As Joe went back down the ladder, Amy looked at Will. "Are you going to go down the ladder?"

"Of course," Will said. "I wouldn't miss a mystery for the world."

As the boys disappeared from sight, Amy looked at her younger sister. "Are you game to go down?"

"Well, I'd rather go with the boys than stay here by ourselves." Sarah sighed. "How come wherever we go we get mixed up in mysteries?"

Amy laughed. "You make it sound as though you don't like them."

"I like them once they're over," Sarah admitted. "I just wish though we could go somewhere and not have a mystery appear."

Amy smiled. "But wouldn't life be boring then?"

"I suppose so." Sarah grabbed hold of the ladder and followed her sister deeper into the mine.

Once the children were all together, Joe swung his torch to the left and then to the right. "I went left last time, so let's go left again." He made his way down the tunnel, stopping shortly after the first bend. He shone the torch towards an alcove. "This is where I hid when I heard the men talking."

"It's a baby cave," Sarah exclaimed.

"Yes, it really is small, so it was fortunate that the men didn't come in, else they would have seen me." After glancing around, Joe resumed walking down the tunnel. When they reached an intersection, he looked at the others. "I can hear voices."

"I think they're coming from the left tunnel," Will said.

"I think so too," Amy whispered.

"Let's only use one torch now." Joe looked at Will. "And proceed slowly. We don't want the men to hear us."

A few minutes later, the children caught sight of a light up ahead. Once it was bright enough to see the tunnel floor, Joe turned off his torch. Walking as quietly as they could, the children slowly advanced towards the light. Getting closer, they saw that the tunnel led into another cave, and this was where the light was coming from.

Joe went as close as he dared to the entrance of the cave before stopping. The others did the same and the group listened to see if they could hear anyone talking. They could, but the voices were too far away for them to hear what was being said.

The children crept closer and, upon reaching the entrance, looked into the cave. The first thing that Will saw were the crates stacked up along the cave walls. There were so many of them. They all had their lids on so he couldn't see what was in them, but he suspected that the contents of the crates would enlighten them as to why these men were in the mine.

A very bright lamp sat on one of the crates at the far end of the cave. This allowed the children to see that there were two more tunnel entrances, both of which were near where the men were sitting.

The children strained their ears in an attempt to hear what was being said, but they couldn't make out a single word. As there was another lamp on the crate between the men, they could see what the two men looked like. They were of average build and one had a bald head while the other had spiked hair.

Amy stared at the man on the left. Sensing that he looked familiar, she whispered to the others. "Isn't that the man who spoke to us in the woods?"

Will studied the bald man. "From this distance it looks as though it could be."

"It must be the same man," Joe stated. "That's why he didn't want to us exploring the wood. He must have thought that if we saw the mine we might stumble upon their secret."

As the bald man looked in their direction, Will shrank back into the dark confines of the tunnel and the others quickly did the same.

Once they had retreated a small distance, Amy looked at the others. "I'm sure that was the man we saw yesterday."

"I didn't like the look of either of those men," Sarah said.

"I wonder why they're down here," Joe muttered.

"Well, if we could look into one of those crates, we might know the answer," Will said.

"But we can't do that while the men are there," Joe said.

Amy looked at the boys. "If you're thinking of waiting until the men leave the cave, we could be here for hours."

"No, I've got a better idea. Just stay here for a moment while I confirm something." Joe crept back to the cave and peered at the crates. He hadn't paid too much attention to them when he had first looked at them, but now he studied them closely.

He grinned to himself. Just as he had suspected, they were stacked next to the walls, but there was a gap. One which was large enough for someone to hide in. And, as the crates were stacked all the way to the other side of the cave, where the men were, the person would be able to get as close as they wanted to hear their conversation.

Joe quickly hurried back to the others. As he told them his plan, Will smiled. "I like that idea."

"I don't," Amy said. "It seems risky."

"Why don't we just tell the police what's going on?" Sarah suggested.

Joe stared at Sarah. "What would be the point in going to the police when we don't know if these men have done anything wrong?"

"So who is going to creep behind the crates?" Will asked, looking at Joe. "You or me?"

"Well, it was my plan, so I'd like to do it," Joe said.

"What shall we do if someone comes down the tunnel?" Sarah asked, worried.

"I'll be back before you know it," Joe reassured his sister.

"You'd better be," Amy replied.

Joe walked back to the cave and silently made his way to the crates. As he crawled into the space, he realised that he would have to take it slowly if he wanted to be quiet.

After crawling for a minute or so, he was able to hear what the men were saying. Wanting to make sure that he didn't miss out on anything, he crept further along, stopping when he saw a space between the crates.

Joe grinned. He was in luck. Now, not only could he hear the men, he could also see them. He looked forward and gazed eagerly at them

Now that he was up close, he saw that the man on the left definitely was the one who had spoken to them yesterday. As for the other man, he was much younger and had spiked hair.

"I'll be glad to get out of this place," Baldy said. "Digging for four weeks is long enough for me."

"I can't imagine working in here for two years like the boss," Spiky said.

A voice suddenly yelled out. "Harold! Derek!"

Spiky looked towards one of the tunnels. "We're here!"

A moment passed and then a man, one who was far more muscular than the other two, emerged from a tunnel and walked over to the two men. "The boss wants a word with all of us."

"Not again!" Spiky complained. "I wonder what he wants this time."

"Well, you can always go back to your old job on the farm," Muscles replied.

Spiky laughed. "No way! Can you imagine how many years I'd have to work there to get the amount of money that I'm going to be getting shortly?"

Baldy stood up. "Come on, we'd better go and see what he wants."

As the three men disappeared down the tunnel from which Muscles had appeared a few minutes earlier, Joe hurried back to the others.

"Where have you been?" Amy asked as she caught sight of her brother. "I thought you were going to be quick."

"I was quick," Joe replied.

"Did you find out why the men are down here?" Will asked.

"Sort of," Joe said. "They talked about digging for a month—"

Sarah frowned. "A month?"

"Yes," Joe said. "As I was saying, they—"

"Isn't that when the hiker disappeared?" Sarah interrupted.

Joe looked at his sister for a moment or two before he grinned. "Of course! The hiker who went missing a month ago was Harold Rodgers."

"Yes, I believe that's what Mrs Olive said," Will replied. "Were the men talking about him?"

Joe shook his head. "No, because he was there in person."

CHAPTER 11

ROTTED AWAY

Will shared a glance with Amy and then looked back at Joe. "How do you know the person you saw was the missing hiker?"

"The man had spiked hair, just like Mrs Olive said," Joe replied.

"I'm sure more than one person has spiked hair," Amy pointed out.

"Probably so," Joe agreed, "but how many have spiked hair and are called Harold?"

"How do you know that's his name?" Will asked.

"Well, after I had been watching the men for a few moments, a man came down the tunnel and yelled out Harold and Derek," Joe replied.

"So the man didn't go missing after all," Sarah said. "He was down here all the time."

Joe nodded. "Yes, which fits in what the men were talking about. They mentioned they had been digging for a month which—"

"Is when the man pretended to go missing!" Will interrupted.

"It was the perfect plan," Joe said. "One that would ensure that everyone stayed away from Claw Mountain as well as the mine."

Amy sighed, looking relieved. "So that probably means that the creature isn't lurking about in the woods."

"Of course it's not. I told you it wasn't still around." Joe suddenly swung around and peered into the blackness of the tunnel.

"Did you hear something?" Amy whispered.

Joe frowned as he saw a light. As the seconds passed, he realised it was getting brighter. "Someone's coming down the tunnel!"

"Oh, no! We'll be discovered," Sarah whispered.

"We can't let that happen," Will said with a determined look on his face.

"We'll have to go down one of the other tunnels, it's our only hope." Joe turned and hurried back into the cave.

"What about hiding in one of these crates?" Amy suggested, walking towards the nearest one.

"No, we don't have time. Come on!" Joe raced across the cave, followed by the others.

Choosing the tunnel on the left, Joe switched on his torch. He knew he was taking a risk, but there was no other choice. He hoped the men wouldn't follow them down this tunnel, but he had no way of knowing.

"Where are we going?" Sarah asked, worried.

"To the ladder," Joe replied. "It's one thing to stop one or two men by ourselves, but we can't stop a whole group of men."

With the glow from Joe's torch lighting the way, the children continued down the winding tunnel. They had no way of knowing where they would end up. All that they could hope for was that they reached the ladder before the men found them.

After a while, they reached an intersection. "Which way shall we go?" As a dim light suddenly appeared on the right, Joe made a snap decision. "Left it is."

The children resumed walking, more quickly than before in case the men who were behind caught up. Reaching another intersection a minute later, Amy suddenly tripped.

Fortunately, Will reached out and stopped her from falling. "Thanks." Amy frowned as she saw what she had tripped over. It was a shovel. "Hey! This must be the first intersection we came across. You know the one that we came to after leaving the ladder?"

Joe looked at his sister. "How can you tell? Everything looks the same to me."

Amy pointed to the shovel. "I remember seeing that earlier on. And, if I recall correctly, it was just after we left the ladder."

Joe glanced at Sarah and Will. "What do you think?"

Will shrugged. "I don't recall seeing the shovel, but if Amy thinks she did, then let's go left and see if she's right."

"Okay," Joe replied.

As Joe turned left and walked down the tunnel, Will looked at him. "I wonder if the men have a map of this mine. I would surely get lost if I was working down here."

"Well, after going back and forth among the tunnels for a month you'd probably get a good sense of where to go," Joe replied.

A few moments later, Sarah triumphantly yelled out. "The baby cave!"

Will smiled as Joe's torch lit up the entrance to the small cave. "You're right."

"Phew! I was getting worried that we were nowhere near the ladder," Joe said.

"Me too," Amy admitted.

The children hurried forward, eager to get out of

the mine once and for all. Arriving at the ladder, Joe switched off his torch and put it into his pocket. As he climbed up, he remembered how the ladder had creaked while climbing down and he hoped nothing would happen to it until all four of them were out of the mine.

Suddenly, just as Sarah was about to follow in his footsteps, one of the rungs that Joe had placed his feet on, broke away. After steadying himself, he glanced down at the others. "Did you see that?"

Amy nodded. "I was holding my breath for a moment there."

"Yes, me too," Joe said. "Fortunately only one rung broke, but there's no knowing how many more have rotted away, so we'd better go up the ladder one at a time. I know it will take a while longer, but if more than one person climbs up at a time, the whole thing might collapse."

"Good thinking," Sarah said. "I'll wait until you say it's okay."

"I'll be as quick as I can." Joe resumed climbing, faster than before. Fortunately, the ladder remained intact and he was soon at the top. After listening for a moment to ascertain if there was anyone about, he called down to the others. "Start climbing."

"Okay, here I come." Sarah started to climb up the ladder. She had almost reached the halfway point when the rung she was holding onto suddenly gave way. She reached out with her hands and tried to grab onto another rung but, before she could get a firm grip on it, the rung that her feet were now on gave way as well.

Sarah tried her best but, as she clung onto one of the rungs with both hands, that also gave way. She cried out in desperation. "Help!"

Amy watched in horror as her sister slid down the ladder as one rung after another gave way. As she realised what was going to happen in a few seconds time, she rushed forward.

Luckily, Will was also quick on his feet and the two of them were able to catch Sarah in their arms.

Joe gazed down in shock. He couldn't believe what he had just witnessed. He knew that the ladder was old, but he hadn't expected half the rungs to disintegrate in just a few seconds. Concerned for his sister, he yelled out. "Are you okay?"

For a moment, no one answered. Then Sarah called out. "My leg's a bit sore, but I'll be alright."

Amy called up to Joe. "We're fine, but the ladder isn't."

"Is there any way you can climb up?" Joe asked.

"No." Amy looked at Will. "We'll have to find another way out of the mine."

Will nodded. "I don't believe that the men we saw were using this hole, so there must be another entrance." He called up to Joe. "Do you have any thoughts about what we should do?"

"Let me think for a moment." Joe sat down on a nearby rock and thought. The ladder was the only way into the mine that they knew of, but he was quite certain there had to be another entrance. He stood up and walked over to the hole.

As he saw the three faces of the others staring up at him, he called down to them. "I can only think of two ways that you can get out."

"What are they?" Amy asked.

"You could search for the other entrance, the one the men are obviously using, or you could wait where you are until I go to the barn and get a rope," Joe said. "I can tie one end to a post up here and then you can pull yourselves up."

Amy looked at the others. "Which suggestion do you like best?"

"Well, searching for the other entrance seems a bit more risky to me, especially since we know that the men are going back and forth in the tunnels right now," Will replied.

"But if we wait here for Joe, someone might come along this tunnel in the meantime and spot us," Sarah piped up.

Will thought for a moment. "If that were to happen, we could make our way to the baby cave as soon as we heard anyone approach."

"But what if they came from the direction of the baby cave?" Amy questioned. "What then?"

"Well, the only thing that I can think of is for us to go to the baby cave straight away and hide there until Joe comes looking for us," Will replied.

Sarah sighed. "If only Mum and Dad were at the farmhouse and not at the hospital."

"Yes, but they're not," Amy said.

"What about getting the police to help?" Sarah asked.

"It's a fifteen minute walk to the village and, even if Joe went there, there's every chance that the constable wouldn't be at the station." Will called up to Joe. "We're going to hide in the baby cave until you get back with the rope."

"So you think that's better than searching for the other entrance?" Joe asked.

"Yes, it's less risky," Will replied. "But be quick."

Joe nodded. "I'll do my best. Oh, you'd better turn off your torch while you wait. You don't want to be stuck down there without any light if the batteries run out."

"Okay, we'll do that," Amy promised.

CHAPTER 12

THE BABY CAVE

Joe hurried down the tunnel and into the cave. He made his way to the hole and crawled out of the mine. He glanced around. No one was in sight.

He started jogging, but soon had to slow down as the snow made it hard work. He took a little longer than he had expected to reach the fence, but he hoped that a few minutes wouldn't matter to the others.

As he hurried down the hill, he looked down at the farmhouse, hoping to see a car, but no vehicle could be seen. As he reached the barn, he heard Jock barking excitedly, anticipating that he would soon be untied.

Joe hurried over to the dog and patted him. "Hello, boy. Now, now, calm down." The dog eagerly licked the boy's face, delighted to see him. "Sorry, Jock, but I have to leave you on this rope for a bit longer. I promise I'll untie you as soon as I can." Leaving the animal, he went into the barn.

He hoped that either the previous owner or Grandpa had left some kind of rope in there. At first, all he saw were some old farm tools, but then he saw a rope. He picked it up, but threw it down again a few moments later. It was only a few feet long, which was far too short.

He kept on searching and, a few minutes later, found another rope. As he uncoiled it, he realised that it was probably long enough, but he took his time studying it. He had to be certain that it was long enough as well as strong enough.

It was one thing for the others to stay in the mine for fifteen minutes, but if he had to go back and get another rope, the chance of the men seeing them would increase considerably.

Joe contemplated searching a while longer in the barn just in case he found a longer rope, but then decided against it. He had to get back to the others. There was no way of knowing how long they could hide in the mine without being noticed by the men. Coiling up the rope, he left the barn and started the journey back to the mine.

~

After sitting in the baby cave for a while, Will switched on his torch and looked at his watch. "It's been fifteen minutes since Joe left us, so he should be back soon. It shouldn't take him long to go to the barn and back."

"He still has to find a rope that's long enough," Amy pointed out.

"I don't think he'll have any trouble doing that," Will said. "After all, most people keep ropes for something or other, and I seem to recall that there were lots of old bits and pieces in the barn."

Sarah looked towards the entrance of the baby cave. "Did you hear something?"

"I thought I did." Will stood up and walked over

to the entrance. He peered into the inky blackness. He could hear nothing and see nothing. He stayed there for a minute, and then walked back to the others. "It must have been my imagination." He sat back down and switched off the torch.

"Can't we have the torch on for a while longer?" Sarah begged. "It's so dark in here when you switch it off."

"But if we have it on all the time the batteries might run out before Joe gets back," Will said. "Besides, if someone were to walk down the tunnel, they would see the light."

Sarah sighed. "I suppose so. I just don't like the dark."

~

Once he arrived back at the ladder, Joe looked down. He listened for a moment to see if he could hear anyone. When he couldn't, he went to work tying one end of the rope around a nearby post.

Satisfied that it would hold the weight of the others, he threw the rest of the rope down into the hole. He then switched his torch on and shone it down the hole to see if the rope had reached the bottom. He breathed a sigh of relief. It had.

Turning off his torch, he put it into his pocket and started climbing down. It was easy going down the hole, but he knew the tough part would be when he had to climb back up. However, with the ladder now out of action, this was the only option and he had to make the best of the situation.

He reached the bottom and was just about to turn on his torch when he stiffened. The sound of voices had reached his ears. Once he had ascertained that they were coming towards him, he quickly climbed back up the rope, going as fast as he could. As he did so, he was careful to hold onto the rope below him. He didn't want the men to see the end of it as they passed as that would be the end of the rescue attempt.

He breathed a sigh of relief as the men walked past. That had been too close. Suddenly, he heard someone yell out.

~

Will stared in shock as the light from the man's torch shone into the baby cave. Even though they had hidden when they had heard the voices, Sarah had been unable to prevent herself from coughing and it had only taken a few seconds for someone to shine a light into the cave and discover the three of them. As the three men walked into the cave, he whispered to the girls. "Let me do the talking."

"What are you kids doing in here?" Muscles growled.

"We got lost in the mine," Will said.

Muscles frowned. "You shouldn't be in this mine. How did you get in here?"

"We climbed down the ladder," Will said.

"What ladder?" Muscles asked.

Will pointed. "Just up ahead on the right. We climbed down, but before we could climb up, it collapsed."

Spiky quickly left the cave. The children waited in silence for twenty seconds before he returned. "They're telling the truth."

Baldy looked at Muscles. "These are the kids that I saw yesterday. I heard them talking about exploring the area and tried to warn them off, but it looks like my talk didn't do any good."

Muscles nodded. "We'll have to tell the boss."

"What about the other kid?" Baldy asked.

Muscles frowned. "What other kid?"

"There was another boy with them yesterday," Baldy replied.

Muscles looked at Sarah. "Where's the other boy?"

"Ahh—" Sarah said.

"At the farmhouse," Will interrupted. "He wanted to stay with the dog."

Muscles looked at Baldy. "Did you see a dog?"

Baldy thinly smiled. "Yes, an ugly brute. It barked at me, that's why I had to show myself. But I don't believe that the boy is at the farmhouse. I think—"

"The boss doesn't pay you to think." Muscles looked at Spiky. "Go and get the boss."

"But he's at the house," Spiky pointed out.

"Then get in the lorry and drive there!" Muscles yelled. He glared at Spiky and Baldy. "Do I need to remind you that the boss put me in charge of things while he's at the house?"

"No, but—" Spiky said.

"But nothing!" Muscles interrupted. "Go and tell the boss,"

"Okay, whatever you say." Spiky left the cave and hurried away.

"If you'll just show us the way out, we'll be on our way," Will said.

"You're not going anywhere until the boss has a talk with you." Muscles glanced at Baldy. "Let's take them to the storage cave." Muscles shone his torch at the children. "Follow me, and don't try any funny business." As the man walked down the tunnel, the children waited to see what Baldy was going to do.

Baldy looked at the children. "Go on! Get going!"

Reluctantly, the three children followed Muscles out of the cave.

~

Joe had been close to being discovered when Spiky had appeared below him but, luckily for him, the man had taken only a quick glance at the bottom of the ladder before he moving on. If he had looked up, everything would have been ruined.

Joe waited for five minutes before he climbed down. After listening intently, he was sure whoever had been in the tunnel earlier was long gone since silence now reigned. He walked down the tunnel towards the baby cave, fervently hoping that the others would still be there. A few moments later, he peered in.

It was empty. Disappointed, Joe sat down and leaned against one of the walls. What was he going to do now? He hadn't thought of a plan in case the others hadn't been there, but he should have. It was all his fault as he had been the one who had suggested going down the ladder. If it hadn't had been for him, none of the others would be missing now. They could have been sitting by the warm fire sipping hot cocoa. Instead, they were probably captured by the men, and it was all because of him.

CHAPTER 13

A MAZE OF TUNNELS

Will soon lost track of where they were going. Even though they had only been walking for about five minutes, he felt hopelessly lost.

Arriving at a medium sized cave, Muscles ushered them inside. As the man had already mentioned the word storage, Will had assumed that the cave would probably contain things that the men were storing in the mine, and he was correct. There were a couple of crates, tins of food and some blankets.

Muscles gave the children a steely glare. "If you behave yourselves and don't cause any trouble, you'll soon be set free." He turned to Baldy. "Guard them until the boss gets here."

"They won't escape while I'm watching them." As Muscles walked away, Baldy looked at the three children. "You might have fooled him with your tale about your friend staying behind, but you didn't fool me. And as soon as the boss gets here, I'll get him to search the mine for him."

"But we told you, he's at the farmhouse," Amy said.

Baldy laughed. "Are you telling me that the boy who seemed the most interested in exploring Claw Mountain stayed behind while you three searched the mine?"

When none of the children replied, Baldy walked over to a crate. He sat down and pulled out a pack of cards.

Amy picked up one of the blankets that was in the corner of the cave and put it around her and her sister. She looked at Will. "Where do you think Joe is?"

Will shrugged his shoulders. "I have no idea."

"I'm scared," Sarah said.

Will put his arm around the girl. "Everything's going to be alright. Just you wait and see."

~

With a sigh, Joe stood up. There was no point sitting in the cave any longer. He had to notify the police. Though he hadn't met the village constable, he was sure he'd be able to help him find the others. The only disadvantage in telling the police was that it would take time, especially since the constable would probably want to wait for backup. And that would take at least half an hour, maybe more. Anything could happen to the others in that time, but what else could he do?

The only other option was to search the mine for the others himself, but if he did that, he'd probably run into the men and get caught as well. If he was lucky and he managed to evade the men, he might find the others, but then he also had a good chance of getting lost.

As he made up his mind to tell the police, he suddenly heard voices. He stiffened and then pressed his body against the side of the cave. He couldn't afford to be seen. He listened intently as the men walked past.

They were talking quickly so he could only catch a few words of what they were saying. But the words that he did hear, cave and children, made him think, What if the others were in the cave with the crates or another cave that he had passed earlier?

As the others had just been caught, Joe realised that if there was ever going to be a time to free them, this was it, for who knew were they might be in an hours time.

He switched on his torch and left the baby cave. He held his torch close to his coat, not wanting to spread too much light in the tunnel in case someone saw it. He also walked softly so that his footsteps wouldn't echo loudly through the tunnel.

He walked slowly, keeping his eyes glued in front of him. As he came to the first intersection, he stopped and looked both ways. As he tried to make up his mind which direction he should head in, he heard voices.

He stood still, wondering if someone was coming down the tunnel towards him. But, as he waited, the voices got quieter. Joe sighed, thankful that whoever he had heard was apparently going in the opposite direction.

However, deciding to play it safe, he walked in the opposite direction. He soon reached another intersection and decided to head left. As far as he recalled, when he had been with the others, they had gone right and hadn't encountered any caves, so he hoped the other direction would provide a better result.

Rounding a corner, he caught sight of a dim light. Walking forward slowly, he realised that it was coming from a cave. He wondered if this was where the others were being held.

There was only one way to know for certain if they were in the cave or not, and that was to peer into it with his own eyes. He switched off his torch, put it into his pocket, and walked forward.

As he got closer, he heard voices. They sounded like the others, but he couldn't be certain. He would need to get a bit closer.

Joe had been so focused on the cave that he had forgotten about the tunnel. Hearing a noise, he whipped towards the left as a light lit up the tunnel. Just a fraction of light reached his feet, but that was enough. A second later, a yell rang out.

Joe grimaced. He turned and hurried back down the tunnel. He had to make it to the rope and out of the mine. As the others were already caught, it was up to him and him alone to get help. He ran as fast as he could, not worrying about the noise that his footsteps made. Now the men knew he was in the mine, it didn't matter how loud he was.

As he reached the intersection and turned down the tunnel that would take him to the rope, he paused in horror. There was a light up ahead.

Joe turned around and looked in the other direction. It was in darkness. He glanced backwards. The man was closing in. He looked down the tunnel that was in the direction of the ladder and saw the glow of a torchlight.

Joe realized there wasn't any use going up a tunnel if there was someone coming down it. So, not liking it, but knowing that it was his only choice, he hurried down the tunnel that was in darkness. He would just have to find another tunnel which led back to the rope.

As he ran, he realized he had made a mistake. Instead of trying to rescue the others, he should have gone straight to the police. If he was caught, all four of them would be imprisoned in the mine. And, to top it all off, no one knew that they were in the mine. No one at all. Not even Jock could save them, for he was tied up at the farmhouse.

Joe put these thoughts aside as he concentrated on the task that lay ahead of him. He tried to form a mental map in his head, but it was too hard. He slowed down as he reached another intersection. Listening, he realised that voices were coming from behind him but not in front of him, which was a good thing. Now he had to make a choice. Left or right?

He chose right as that seemed to lead in the direction of the hole. He knew that most tunnels twisted and turned, but he hoped this wouldn't be the case for this particular one. Luckily for him, it wasn't.

Five minutes later, he caught sight of the hole. He had made it! But was the rope still where he had left it? It was, thankfully. After taking one more look around him to make sure that there was no sign of the men, he put his torch back into his pocket and started the climb upward.

Joe breathed a sigh of relief as his hands clasped the top of the hole. He had done it! He was tempted to rest for a few minutes as the run in the tunnels had partially exhausted him, but he knew that if he did, all the effort that he had just made might be for nothing.

He had made the mistake of not informing the police earlier when he had the chance, but he wasn't going to make the same mistake twice. There would be no joy in having the police come to the mine only to discover that the others could not be found.

Determined to make up for his wrong judgement call earlier, he stood up and hurried into the main cave. As he did so, a light was suddenly shone in his eyes. He froze. As the light left his face and he glanced in the direction from which it was coming, he saw a man. It was Muscles!

CHAPTER 14

THE MEETING

Muscles had a broad grin on his face. "Look what we have here!"

Joe was disappointed with himself. It was obvious that the man had lain in wait for him, but instead of waiting at the bottom of the hole, he had waited at the top. He put his hands up in mock surrender. As he saw the man relax, he took off running towards the mine entrance.

Muscles rushed after Joe, grasping the boy's arm with his burly hand.

"Ow! Let me go!" Joe yelled. He struggled to get away from the man's grasp, but he couldn't.

Muscles grinned smugly at the boy. "I'm not going to let go of you until you're with the others."

"Why do you want to keep us locked up?" Joe questioned. "If you let us go, we won't tell a single person that you're in the mine."

Muscles laughed. "I'm no fool. You'll promise one thing, but when you get out of here you'll change your mind. Come on, let's get moving." He pushed Joe towards the hole.

"Where are we going?" Joe asked.

"We're going back down the hole so you can be

reunited with your friends," Muscles replied.

A smile flickered across Joe's face. If he was able to go down first, then the man wouldn't be able to stop him and he'd be able to run down one of the tunnels. And, if the man went first, he could run away. Trying not to show that he was happy about what was about to happen, Joe looked at the man. "So who's going to go down first?"

"You are. But I'll need you to give me your torch," Muscles said.

Joe frowned. "My torch?"

Muscles nodded and held out his hand. "Give it to me. Now."

"I didn't bring one with me," Joe lied.

Muscles laughed. "Do you think I'm stupid? Do you want me to make you give it up or are we going to do this peacefully?"

Joe hesitated. If he had a torch, it may have been possible to lose the man in the many tunnels that made up the mine but, without it, he wouldn't stand a chance. He reluctantly reached into his pocket and handed over his torch.

"Now, down the rope." Muscles looked at his watch. "Come on, we don't have all day."

Joe walked over to the hole and climbed down. The man waited a minute before he followed the boy. Once the two of them were down on solid ground again, the man pushed the boy down the tunnel. "Get going and hurry up. I haven't got time to waste."

The two of them walked down the tunnel for roughly five minutes before they came in sight of a light coming from within a cave. It was the same one that Joe had seen light coming from earlier.

Walking into the medium sized cave, Joe saw that the others were standing by the wall at the back.

He walked over to them and noticed the look of disappointment on their faces. But he didn't take it personally. He was sure they had been hoping that he would come back with the police.

Before he could exchange words with the others, Muscles walked over to them. "Don't get any fancy ideas about trying to escape. The boss will be here soon and then you'll discover what happens to kids who go where they shouldn't." He turned to Baldy. "Make sure they don't escape."

"They're not going to escape under my watch." As Muscles left, Baldy turned to the children. "You can talk amongst yourselves, but keep it quiet."

"Can we sit down on that mattress over there?" Sarah pleaded, pointing.

The man grudgingly nodded. "Okay."

The children moved over to the mattress and sat down. For the next few minutes, Joe filled the others in on everything that had happened to him since they had split up.

Once he had finished talking, Amy glanced at the man. Satisfied that he couldn't hear them, she whispered to the others. "So, does anyone have any ideas about how we can get out of here?"

"The boss might let us go once he sees that we're just children," Sarah said, hopeful.

"I don't think so," Will said. "But, as my father likes to say, you can never have too much hope. So let's all hope that the boss will let us go."

The children fell silent as they contemplated the situation that they were in. A few minutes had passed before Baldy, who had been leaning against the cave entrance, suddenly yelled out. "Up on your feet you lot! The boss is here."

The children quickly stood up. As much as Joe

feared what the boss was going to say to them, it was better than sitting in the cold cave not knowing what their future held. He looked at the others. "Let me do the talking."

A moment later, the boss entered. He was tall and had short brown hair. A long scar cut across the right side of his face. He was dressed in dirty clothes and wore black gloves. He limped towards the four children and studied each of them in turn.

"If you don't let us go, the police will be coming to find us," Sarah burst out.

"Oh they will, will they?" The boss peered at the small girl. "So you told your parents you were going to explore an old, deserted mine, did you?"

"Yes," Sarah lied, putting on a brave face.

The boss grinned smugly at the girl. "You're lying." He turned to Will. "Why did you come here?"

"We thought it would be fun," Will said. "We like exploring old places."

"You do, do you?" The boss laughed. "Then you won't mind if we keep you with us for two days."

"Two days!" Amy exclaimed. "You can't keep us here for that long."

"You'll do as you're told!" The boss yelled.

"The longer you keep us down here, the more worried our parents are going to be," Joe said. "And if they start searching—"

"Nobody's going to find you down here," the boss interrupted. "I can't disrupt my plans because of you and, since I don't know what you've seen or what you've heard, I can't take a chance on letting you go. I can't have anyone coming into this mine, especially not tonight or tomorrow."

Joe shared a glance with Will before turning his attention back to the boss. "Is that when you're leaving?

Tomorrow night?"

The man glared at Joe. "That's none of your business. When I do, I'll leave a note for the local constable so that you don't starve. But no funny business." The boss looked at Spiky who had accompanied him to the cave. "Go and get some food and water. We'll keep them here until darkness falls and then we'll move them to the house."

"Why don't we move them now?" Spiky argued.

"Because I'm the boss and I'm the one who makes the plans." The boss turned to the four children. "I'm going to leave now, but I'll see you when you arrive at the house."

As Spiky and the boss left the cave, Baldy looked at the children. "I'm not a fan of keeping children locked up—"

"Then let us go!" Sarah pleaded.

"You can tell the boss that you were taking a nap and we escaped," Amy suggested.

Baldy shook his head. "Orders are orders. You should have listened to me when I told you to stay away from Claw Mountain." He took the chair he had been sitting on earlier and put it in the middle of the cave entrance. "I'm going to rest for a while, so don't shout or yell." As the man closed his eyes, the children sat back down on the mattress.

CHAPTER 15

PRISONERS

Amy sighed. "I wish we had told someone where we were going."

"Mum and Dad will know something has happened when they come back from the hospital," Sarah said.

"How will they know? They might think that we went for a walk." Amy gazed up at the roof of the cave. "By the time they realise that something has happened to us it will be evening. And by then who knows where we'll be."

"But even if they searched straight after they came home, why would they search the mine?" Joe questioned. "That's probably the last place that they would look."

"Actually, if they thought that we were mixed up in another mystery, they might search the mine first," Amy replied.

"Possibly," Will said. "You know your parents better than I do, but even if they did search the mine, they'd have to climb down the hole if they were going to find us. And, as I doubt that the rope is still there, I can't see them getting another rope just on the slight chance that we were down here."

"The rope might still be there," Sarah said.

Will shook his head. "I don't think so. Whatever these men are up to, it's clear to me that they are smart enough to make sure that no one finds us until they're ready to leave. That's why they're not taking the chance of moving us until nightfall. So I can't imagine that they would leave something in one of the upper caves that would indicate to anyone that someone was down here. Untying the rope would probably have been the first thing that the boss would have done after he left us."

"Anyone can slip up now and then," Amy pointed out.

Sarah stared at the ground. "If only Jock was here."

"What could Jock do against all these men?" Amy questioned.

"I don't know, but it would be something," Sarah replied. "Anything is better than nothing. But since Joe tied him up, he couldn't come searching for us even if he wanted to."

"But even if he wasn't tied up, he wouldn't find his way down here," Joe said. "He's smart, but no dog is going to leap down the hole that we climbed down. I know there must be another entrance, but if we haven't found it, it can't be that easy to find."

"So we're trapped," Sarah muttered.

Joe shook his head. "Nothing is impossible. I'm sure if we all think hard, we'll be able to find a way to get out of here."

Will looked around at the cave. Apart from the crates and the mattress, all he could see was the chair that the man was sitting on and an oil lamp that sat on one of the crates. "I can't see anything here that we could use to help us escape."

"So what do we do then?" Amy questioned.

"I don't know, but we need to think of something,"

Joe replied. "It's possible that it might be easier to escape when they take us to the house, but I wouldn't count on it."

"We could do as the men say and wait for them to release us," Sarah said.

"But we don't know when that's going to be," Joe argued. "We could be locked up forever."

"When do you think Mum and Dad will be coming home?" Amy questioned.

"Well, they could already be home," Joe replied. "I didn't ask how far away the hospital was. I know they said they'd be two or three hours, but we don't know how long they would have to wait until the doctor examined Grandma."

The children fell silent as Spiky came into the cave. He handed Joe a plate with some bread on it. "Here." He then placed a jug of water on the floor. "I'll be back later to collect the dishes."

"Where are the glasses?" Amy asked.

"The last one broke yesterday so you'll have to drink out of the jug," Spiky said.

"But we can't—" Sarah protested.

"Don't argue. Just be glad you're getting something to eat and drink." Spiky turned and walked away.

Joe looked at the bread and water. "Well, it's not much, but I suppose it's better than nothing."

Will took hold of the bread and tried breaking it into pieces. He grimaced. "It seems rock hard." A few seconds later, he managed to break a piece off. He handed the rest of the bread to Amy.

Amy shook her head. "No, thank you. It doesn't look too appetizing so I think I'll wait until I get hungry before I have some. Besides, sitting in this cold cave has made me stop thinking about food."

Joe put his hand out. "I'll try the bread."

Despite the grim situation, Amy smiled as her brother took the bread from Will. "I don't think anything would put you off food, would it?"

"Of course not, why should it?" Joe smiled as he broke the bread in half. "After all, it's always darkest just before the dawn."

Sarah frowned. "But dawn is hours away."

"I'm not talking about the actual dawn," Joe explained. "It's just a saying."

"What does it mean?" Sarah asked.

"Well, when things look bleak, just hold on because sooner or later things will improve," Joe replied.

"My dad likes to use that saying too," Will said. "Though, the situations that he has been in when he said it have not been as dark as this, but the saying still rings true."

"Just because it's a saying doesn't mean that it's true," Amy pointed out.

"No, but it doesn't mean that it's not true," Joe replied. "Anyway, the reason I said that was to lighten the mood. You can never predict the future so let's get some rest and see what happens in a few hours. Who knows, by that time the police might be raiding the mine."

The four children lay down on the mattress and closed their eyes. But sleep evaded them. Their minds were too busy thinking about what was going to happen. Finally, after several hours, the girls managed to get some sleep. Then Will also fell asleep.

But try as he might, Joe couldn't. Feeling stiff from lying in the cramped space, he sat up and got off the mattress.

Wanting to stretch his legs, he paced back and forth along the cave wall. He did this for some time, trying to think of how he and the others could get out of the situation they were in. But nothing came to him. It was one thing to be held hostage in a manor, like the one they had been in during their very first adventure, but this was the worst place they had ever been held in.

There was only one way out of this cave and that was blocked by the bald man. He didn't want to admit it to the others, but he couldn't think of how they could escape. His only hope was that the house that the men planned to take them to later on would be easier to escape from.

There was also a chance that they could do something while they were being taken from the mine to the house. Being a keen reader, Joe had read numerous books about people escaping from their captors while travelling in a vehicle. However, none of the stories had been based on fact, so he didn't know if this would work in their situation, but at least it was something to think about.

He walked back to the mattress and lay down again. He closed his eyes, but still he couldn't sleep. Even though he was wearing a coat, he still felt cold in the cave. He glanced at his watch from time to time and, as the minutes turned into hours, he wondered how long it would be before someone came to take them to the house.

He suddenly heard a noise. He sat up and gazed curiously at the cave entrance. He thought he had heard a bark. A moment later, he heard another bark. As the barking continued, the others sat up and glanced around.

"Is that a dog?" Amy asked.

Sarah's green eyes gleamed in delight as the barking got louder. "It must be Jock!"

"I don't see how that's possible," Will said. "It's most

likely a dog that belongs to one of the men."

The children listened as the barking became louder. Baldy opened his eyes and stood up. He looked out of the cave, trying to see where the noise was coming from. A few moments passed and then, as well as the barking, they heard several men yelling out.

Baldy glanced at the children. "Don't move." He turned and, flicking his torch on, made his way out of the cave.

"It must be Jock!" Sarah exclaimed. "The man wouldn't have left us like that if one of them owned a dog."

Joe turned to the others. "Now's our chance! Quickly, before he returns!"

CHAPTER 16

ESCAPE

The children rushed to the cave entrance and looked out. Darkness greeted them. Will sighed. "How can we? We don't have a torch. The men took them."

"We'll take the lamp." Joe hurried over to where the oil lamp was sitting on one of the crates and picked it up. He also picked up the box of matches that was beside it before making his way out of the cave. Remembering that the bald man had gone to the right, he went left.

They had been walking down the tunnel for less than a minute when Will glanced behind him and frowned as he spotted a glow of a torch light following them. "It must be the bald man. Let's speed up, we don't want to be spotted."

However, even the increase in speed didn't do any good as, a few moments later, a yell rang out. Will looked behind him and caught sight of the torchlight. It was closer than before. "Run!"

With the lamp bobbing back and forth, the group raced down the tunnel. Reaching an intersection, Joe went to the left.

As the chase continued in earnest, Joe turned down a tunnel that they hadn't explored as he attempted to lose the man. As he spotted an alcove on the left of him, he glanced at the others. "Let's hide in here and wait for the man to pass. If we turn out the lamp, hopefully he won't spot us. Amy, how many matches are there in this box?" He pulled the box from his pocket and handed it to his sister.

Amy quickly opened the box of matches. "It's half full."

"Good. I'll turn the light out now." As darkness swept the area, Joe whispered to the others. "Keep as still as you can."

Once the man had passed, the children breathed a sigh of relief. They waited for a few moments to make sure that he had gone before they decided it was time to get moving.

A match was lit and, moments later, the lamp was burning brightly once more. They left the alcove and made their way back up the tunnel.

Reaching the intersection, Joe paused. "Let's take the tunnel to the right just in case there's someone else following the man."

"But then it will take longer to get to the hole," Sarah protested.

"Hadn't we better search for the entrance that the men use?" Will asked. "I doubt that the rope will still be there."

"It probably won't be, but it's worth checking," Joe said.

Amy nodded. "I agree, but I think we should go straight there. Once the man behind us realises that he's lost us, he'll report back to the boss. Once that happens, everyone will be on the lookout for us."

Joe resumed the trek down the tunnel and, since they didn't encounter anyone, they soon arrived at the hole. They eagerly looked upwards, but gave a groan of dismay as they saw that the rope was no longer there.

Disappointed, Joe turned to the others. "We'll have to find the entrance that the men use."

"But how are we going to do that?" Sarah exclaimed. "We haven't the faintest idea which tunnel leads to the entrance."

"No, but we've been along a lot of them and we haven't found any way out of the mine," Joe said. "So, the tunnel we're looking for must be one that we haven't explored."

Amy suddenly turned to Joe. "You know that cave that we saw those crates in?"

Joe nodded. "Yes, what about it?"

"Well, wouldn't you think that if the men placed those crates there, it would be fairly close to the entrance?" Amy asked.

Will frowned. "What do you mean?"

"If you were using a cave as a storage room for the crates, wouldn't it make sense to choose one that was close to the entrance?" Amy questioned. "That way, once the crates were filled, you wouldn't have a long distance to carry them."

Will nodded. "That makes sense."

"Let's go to the cave and choose a tunnel that we haven't gone down," Amy suggested. "It might not lead anywhere, but I think there's a good chance it will lead out of this mine."

The children resumed walking back down the tunnel. They arrived at the storage cave and looked in. There was no one in sight, so they made their way across the cave and towards the tunnel that was on the far side.

They had just reached it when Joe stopped. "Wait!" He hurried forward. He was back in a few moments with a grim face. "There's someone coming towards us."

"We'll have to head down another tunnel," Amy said.

"No! Let's hide instead," Will said. "Then, once the men pass, we can go down the tunnel that they came from. I don't know about you, but I'm sick of these tunnels and I don't want to keep on running forever."

"Hide where?" Sarah asked. "There's nothing in here except crates."

"Maybe we can hide behind them." Will hurried over to the crates and looked behind them. He sighed. "I don't think all of us would be able to fit."

"What if we hide in them?" Joe suggested.

"What a good idea! Let's see if we can get the lids off." Will glanced towards the tunnel. "Come on, the men will be here any moment."

With everyone helping, it only took a few seconds to take off the lid of the nearest crate. They all peered into it. Rocks filled most of the container.

Will grinned. "Of course! That's what the men are doing. They're stealing the gold before the mine reopens next month."

Amy nodded. "Yes, you're probably right. Hey, what if we took out some of the rocks and put them into another crate?"

"But that will take time," Will said.

Joe raced towards the tunnel and listened. He could hear the men arguing. He couldn't hear the specifics, but if the men wanted to yell and shout at one another then that was okay with him. As long as it bought them time, that was all that mattered. He hurried back to the others. "The men are arguing, so if we're quick, we may just have enough time."

While the girls took off the lids, the boys carried the rocks from one crate to another. With everyone working as fast as they could, it wasn't long before they had almost emptied four of the crates.

Amy quickly whipped her head towards the tunnel. "I hear voices!"

"Quick! Into the crates!" Joe waited for a moment for the others to climb into the crates before extinguishing the lamp. He then placed it behind one of the crates, hoping that the men wouldn't notice it.

He had just climbed into his crate and was putting the lid on when Baldy and Spiky entered the cave. Spotting a small hole in the side of his crate, he peered through it and saw the men approach the crates.

"Let's check behind the crates," Baldy said. "I doubt there's room, but kids are pretty small."

As the men walked over, Joe hoped that they wouldn't notice the lamp. The men didn't say anything for a few moments as they inspected the wall but then, as they headed towards another pile of crates, Spiky stopped and walked over to his crate. "What's this?"

Joe realised Spiky had found the lamp. He could only hope that he thought it had been left by one of the other men.

"It's only a lamp," Baldy said.

"I know that," Spiky replied. "But what's it doing on the floor?"

"I don't know," Baldy said. "Come on, let's go and report back to the boss."

"But don't you think—" Spiky muttered.

"Think what?" Baldy interrupted. "That the children came into this cave and left that lamp there?"

Spiky nodded. "Yes."

"And why would they do that? We know they don't have any torches, that's why they took the lamp," Baldy said. "So if they were the ones who left that lamp here, they would be left with no light." He laughed. "The next thing you'll be telling me is that they put the lamp there because they decided to hide in these crates."

"That's actually not such a bad thought," Spiky said.

Baldy frowned. "What? You think that was a serious suggestion?"

Spiky shook his head. "No, but now I think about it, it could be true."

"Really? Look, I'll show you." Baldy walked over to a crate and pried the lid off. "See? There's no one here." He placed the lid back on and walked away. "Come on, let's get going."

"But what about the other crates?" Spiky questioned.

Baldy threw up his hands. "If you want to check every single crate, be my guest, but I'm going."

Joe watched anxiously as he saw Spiky glance around at the crates. If the man stayed and inspected them, there was no doubt in his mind that he and the others would be found.

CHAPTER 17

SEPERATED

Fortunately, Spiky followed the bald man out of the cave. Joe breathed a sigh of relief. That had been too close. After waiting for a few moments, he pushed the lid off his crate. As it was completely dark inside the cave, he couldn't see the others as they emerged from the other crates, but he could hear them.

Suddenly, a light flared as Amy struck a match. "Where did you put the lamp? I can't see it."

Joe sighed, disappointed. "One of the men took it."

"What?" Will spluttered. "How do you know?"

Joe explained about the hole in his crate. As he finished talking, Sarah looked at the others. "What are we going to do now?"

"Without a light we can't do anything," Will replied.

"We may as well give up then," Amy said.

"No! No one's going to be giving up," Joe said. "It will be slower, but…" He suddenly stopped and listened. "There's someone coming!" He looked towards one of the tunnels where a dim light could be seen. As the light got brighter, he turned to the others. "Quick! Back in the crates."

The children hastily climbed back into the crates and put the lids on. They had just finished doing so when the men entered the cave.

Through the small hole, Joe saw that there were four men. He wondered why there were so many and then, with a shock, he realised there was only one answer. They hadn't come searching for them, they were here for the crates!

He sat as still as he could as the men started to carry the crates out of the cave. His crate was one of the first that they chose.

Joe wondered if all the crates were going to be taken out. If so, this could be their chance to escape. Either way, this was better than being locked up in the house that the boss had said they were going to be taken to. As long as his lid wasn't nailed down, he could escape at any time.

As the noise of a vehicle reached his ears, he realised he must be getting close to the entrance of the mine. Peering through the hole, he saw darkness. He wondered if he was still in the mine, but then he saw the outline of a lorry up ahead.

Even with the moon overhead and one of the men holding a lamp near the lorry, Joe couldn't see much. Just some trees and snow, that was all. His body slammed against the side of the crate as the men loaded it onto the vehicle. He was sure he was going to be getting a few bruises from this experience but, if that was all he got, it would be okay.

He sat still as he heard more crates being placed into the lorry. Then, as the voices ceased and the sound of footsteps faded away, he wondered what was going to happen next. He didn't have to wonder for too long as, a moment later, he heard footsteps approach the vehicle.

Seconds later, a man yelled out. It was Muscles. Joe then heard a door open and shut. As the engine roared to life, he realised that he was going to be driving the vehicle. While he was wondering if there was only going to be one man delivering the crates, he heard footsteps approach the back of the lorry.

Peering through the small hole in the crate, he saw two men clamber aboard. As they sat down, he could no longer see through the hole. With a shock, he realised that one of the men was sitting on his crate! He froze. All it was going to take for the man to stand up and pull away the lid was for him to sneeze or cough.

Joe closed his eyes and tried to relax. In doing so, he hoped to lessen the noise of his breathing. It would be such a shame if the men discovered him now.

As the lorry rumbled down the dirt road, Joe was in two different mindsets. On one hand he was excited to be finally leaving the mine, but on the other hand he was dismayed that his chance of escaping could come crashing down at any moment.

All he could hope for was that the journey wasn't going to take long. Luckily for him, it didn't. Five to ten minutes later, the vehicle came to a stop. As soon as it did, the man stood up and climbed out of the lorry. The other man did the same.

Joe heard the driver's door open and slam shut a moment later. Not knowing if the men were going to unload the crates, he kept still.

As the voices began to get quieter and quieter, he relaxed. It looked as though luck was on his side. Once he was sure he couldn't hear anyone, he slowly removed the lid and stood up. As he glanced around, a lid from a nearby crate was removed. Joe smiled as Will poked his head out. "Hey!"

Will smiled back. "It's good to see you. As soon as I heard those two men climb aboard just before we left the mine, I grew worried. I was afraid I might sneeze and then they would find me."

"Those were my thoughts too," Joe said. "Especially when one of the men sat on my crate."

Will looked shocked. "He did?"

Joe grimly smiled. "Yes." He stepped out of his crate and walked to the rear of the vehicle. Though it was dark, the full moon allowed him to see that the lorry was parked at the end of a long driveway. Looking to the left, he saw a small house. It was aglow with lights. "That must be where the men went."

"Which means that we can escape," Will said.

Joe nodded. "Let's tell the girls and get out of here." He glanced around at the crates and whispered. "Amy? Sarah?" As no one answered, he turned to Will. "You don't think they're still back at the cave, do you?"

"Why would they be?" Will questioned. "Maybe one of the men nailed down some of the lids and that's why they haven't climbed out."

"That doesn't explain why they don't answer." Joe walked further into the lorry and whispered yet again. "Amy? Sarah?" Still no one answered. He frowned. "I don't like the look of this. Let's remove the lids."

Joe went to work removing the nearest lid. As soon as he saw that it contained nothing but rocks, he moved on to the next one. Will helped him and, soon, there was just one crate left.

Joe pried the lid off and peered in. "Rocks!" He kicked the wood in frustration. "Blow!"

Will sighed and sat down. "You were right. They're not here."

Joe paced back and forth. "I don't understand. How can that be?"

"I don't know," Will admitted. "Maybe they only take a certain number of crates from the mine each time."

"But the lorry is only half full," Joe said.

Will stood up. "Let's get out of here and notify the police. They'll be able to find the girls wherever they are."

"I just don't understand it." Joe was about to say something else when he heard a noise. He frowned. "That sounds like a plane." He hurried to the back of the lorry and peered out.

At first, all he could see were the stars and the moon but then, as Will joined him, he saw something sweep across the moon. It was an aeroplane.

"So that's what they're waiting for." Hearing voices, Joe looked towards the house and saw the glow of a torch. "They're coming back. Quick, before they get here."

Joe slid down onto the ground. He was about to run down the driveway when he saw a flicker of light. "Blow!" He quickly glanced around, hoping to spot some bushes that he and Will could hide behind. But all he could see was grass. He climbed back into the lorry. "It's too risky to escape now."

"Can't we hide somewhere in the garden?" Will asked.

"No. We'll have to wait for the next chance we get," Joe replied.

The two boys hurried to the back of the lorry and climbed into the same two crates that they had hidden in previously.

Joe had just pulled the lid over his crate when he heard the door of the lorry open. A few moments later, the engine sprung to life and two men climbed into the back of the lorry. The vehicle then reversed down the driveway.

CHAPTER 18

THE NIGHT FLIGHT

As the lorry sped down the road, Joe wondered how long this trip would take. He didn't think it would be long and he was correct. Roughly five minutes later, the lorry turned off the main road and rumbled onto a dirt road. It came to a stop a minute later.

As the driver opened his door, a voice yelled out. "What took you so long? I want to get away before the storm hits."

"What storm?" Muscles asked. "I can't see anything."

"You'll soon see plenty if you don't get those crates unloaded quickly," the first voice said.

Moment's later, the crate that Joe was in suddenly moved. He was flung from side to side as the men pulled his crate out of the lorry. Remembering the small hole that he had looked through earlier, he peered through it. He couldn't see much due to the darkness, but he could see the full moon as well as a few lamps that were scattered on the grassy field.

As he saw the lorry parked right next to an aeroplane, he realised that it had to be the one that had passed over the house earlier. It all made sense. Muscles had driven to the house and waited in the warm confines of the building until he'd heard the plane fly overhead.

He glimpsed a man whom he assumed to be the pilot and he was able to see part of the plane as the men carried his crate into the machine. The men placed the crate down near the back of the plane and hurried back to get the rest of the crates.

As the aeroplane engine started up a minute later, he realised that escape would have to wait until the plane landed. The plane taxied along the grass, gained speed, and then took off.

As the machine levelled off and turned to the right, Joe listened carefully. Once he was sure that that he couldn't hear anyone nearby, he pushed off the lid.

Due to the many lights that lit up the inside of the plane, he was able to see a good deal. His crate, along with the rest of the crates, was at the rear of the plane. There was an open doorway that led to the front of the plane. Peering down the aisle, he saw seats. This would be where the passengers would sit but, luckily for him, it was completely devoid of people. Past these seats was a closed door. He assumed that this led to the cockpit.

He climbed out of his crate, wondering if Will was inside one of the other crates. Suddenly, one of the lids moved and out poked Will's head. Joe breathed a sigh of relief. "I was hoping we'd still be together."

"Me too." After he glanced down the aisle and saw that the door to the cockpit was closed, Will looked at Joe. "Any idea where we are?"

"I haven't had a chance to look yet," Joe replied.

The two of them walked over to the window and glanced out. Darkness greeted them. Will sighed. "I thought we might see some lights from buildings but, since we can't, that must mean we're flying over a deserted area."

A moment later, lightning lit up the sky. As thunder

crackled overhead, Joe remembered that the pilot had been concerned about a storm. As more lightning lit up the sky, he saw they were flying over a mountainous region that was heavily wooded. "Where do you think we're going?"

"I don't know," Will admitted. "Looking at the mountain peaks below, it seems to me that we're heading somewhere that's even more remote than Claw Mountain."

"Couldn't they be flying in this direction to avoid the storm?" Joe questioned.

"If that was their plan, they don't seem to be doing a good job of it," Will replied. "From the looks of it, it seems as though the storm is getting closer."

For the next few minutes, both boys peered out of the window as the rain pelted against the glass. Thunder rattled overhead and sheet lightning caused the sky to light up so that it almost looked as though it was the middle of the day.

Suddenly, a massive streak of forked lightning hit the aircraft. The boys were thrown to the ground as the machine shuddered. Joe tried to stand up, but the plane was twisting and weaving so much he couldn't. He fell back down again and grabbed hold of a crate to steady himself. Will did the same.

As soon as the pilot managed to stabilize the aircraft, Joe froze with fear. The right wing was ablaze!

Before Joe could say anything, Will joined him at the window. His face turned pale. "If the flames spread, the pilot will have no choice but to land the plane."

"But how can he?" Joe gazed down at the trees below. "There's no flat area in sight. Just trees and more trees."

"It's either that or wait until the whole aircraft catches alight," Will muttered.

Joe frowned as the aircraft started to descend. "It

looks as though you're right."

Will quickly glanced around. "We'll need to find something to hang onto. If the pilot lands this plane, we'll be tossed about like rag dolls."

Joe suddenly looked at Will. "The seats. We should strap ourselves into them and put our heads down. That should be the safest."

"But what if the men see us?" Will asked.

"Let's see if the door to the cockpit is closed. If it isn't, we won't be able to do that." Joe hurried to the cargo door and slowly opened it. He breathed a sigh of relief. "It's closed." He hurried forward, Will following close behind.

As the aircraft continued to descend at an alarming rate, the boys stumbled towards the row of seats and strapped themselves in.

As the aircraft hurtled towards the ground, there was no doubt in Joe's mind that the pilot had lost control. For all he knew, the lightning bolt which had struck the plane might have also damaged the controls, which might have led to the engine dying.

Joe could only hope that the pilot managed to find a place to land that wasn't completely covered by trees. He didn't even want to think about what would happen if the front of the plane smashed into the trunk of a tree.

As the plane slammed into the ground, glass shattered and one of the wings was ripped away from the fuselage. Thankfully, a few moments later, the aircraft came to a shuddering stop. The lights switched off straight away as the engine died, but there was enough moonlight coming through the windows for the two boys to see each other.

Joe turned to his friend. "Are you okay?"

"Yes, I'm fine," Will replied. "Let's get out of here

before the men see us."

They hurried down the aisle and, as Joe opened the door, he saw a large gaping hole on the right side of the cabin where the emergency door had been. "Golly. Imagine if we had been in here when that happened. We might have been blown out."

Will nodded. "We're fortunate to have survived the crash without any injuries."

"Yes, but now we need to find out where we are so we can decide what's the best thing to do." Joe paced back a forth for a few moments as he thought. He suddenly turned towards the cabin door. He opened it a tad and peered through. He shut it immediately. "The men are coming!"

CHAPTER 19

FOLLOW THE LEADER

Will quickly looked around. "Let's go through this hole."

Joe followed Will as they made their way out into the snow. Since it was dark and they had no torch, they didn't venture too far. After walking towards the tail of the aeroplane, they crouched down in the shadows just as a light appeared as one of the men shone a torch around the cabin.

A few moments later, Muscles stepped out into the snow. The man glanced around before he rejoined his companion in the cabin.

"The boss isn't going to be happy about this," Muscles growled.

"Good thing we're nearly finished," the pilot replied.

"Nearly finished isn't good enough," Muscles stated. "How do you propose to deliver the rest of the gold?"

"By lorry," the pilot answered.

"The boss wouldn't like that," Muscles said. "If the police stopped the vehicle for any reason, how is the driver going to explain the gold?"

"He can make something up off the top of his head," the pilot replied. "Besides, after this load, there was only going to be two more before we've finished."

As the two men continued to talk, Joe studied the landscape. Although the sky was cloudy, the full moon gave enough light for him to see the lay of the land. All he could see were trees, trees and more trees. Thunder still rumbled in the distance, but it didn't bother him as the storm was obviously moving away.

As Joe heard the men walk back down the aisle, he turned to Will. "What we need most is what those men had, which is a torch."

"There might be another torch in the plane. Come on, let's see." Will walked back into the cabin and started searching while Joe kept watch.

Fortunately, with the full moon lighting up the cabin, there was enough light to enable Will to find a torch in less than a minute. He slipped it into his pocket and walked over to Joe. "I found one."

"Does it work?" Joe asked.

Will switched it on. "Yes." He immediately switched it off again, not wanting to waste the batteries. "Now that we have a torch, what's the plan?"

"Well, if we knew where we were, we could walk to the nearest town," Joe replied. "But I haven't the faintest idea where we are."

Will shook his head. "I don't know either. For all I know, we could be in Wales."

Joe frowned. "That's a long way from Claw Mountain, and we weren't in the air for very long, so I don't think so."

"But we don't know how fast the aeroplane was going," Will pointed out. "Or in which direction." He slumped down onto one of the crates. "We might only be a ten minute walk from the nearest town and yet we're never going to know."

"Well, there's one thing for certain," Joe said.

"What's that?" Will asked.

"The pilot knows where we are," Joe replied. "He must carry a map in the cockpit and, even if he didn't, if he had flown along this route previously, he would probably know the area by heart anyway."

"But what's the good of that?" Will argued. "It's not as though we can just walk up to him and ask where the nearest police station is."

"I know that, but there's nothing to stop us from listening in on their conversation," Joe said. "Then, once we learn which way to go, we can head off before the men."

"That might work." Will peered down the aisle and saw the two men walking towards them. He quickly shrank back. "They're coming back!"

Trying to make as little noise as possible, Will and Joe leapt out into the snow again and hid once more. A few moments later, the men walked into the cabin. From the sounds that were being made, they seemed to be searching for something.

Muscles sighed. "It isn't here."

"It must be," the pilot muttered. "Maybe it got knocked to the ground due to the rough landing."

"It mustn't have been put back after you took it out on the previous flight," Muscles said.

"Maybe if we search the cockpit again we'll find it," the pilot suggested.

"No, we've wasted enough time. Anyway, one torch ought to do us," Muscles replied. "I'd rather take a chance with one torch than wait around in this cold weather searching for something that may not even be here. The sooner I'm back at the house warming my feet by the fire the better."

As the glow from the torch diminished, Joe breathed a sigh of relief. He looked at Will. "Let's wait a minute to make sure that they've gone."

The boys waited in silence and then, after a minute had passed, they re-entered the cabin.

Joe looked down the aisle to see if he could see the men. For the first time he could see straight into the cockpit. He frowned. "I think they've gone. They must have already looked at the map and decided which direction to head in."

Will hurried to the window and looked out. He spotted a flash of light through the trees for a moment or two before it disappeared. "We'll have to hurry! We can't afford to lose them."

Leading the way, Joe switched on his torch and hurried out of the plane. He knew that the men would see the light if they turned around, but there was nothing he could do about it. Without the light, they might stumble over a fallen tree branch or a rock.

The men weren't wasting any time and it took the boys two to three minutes to catch up to them. Once they had, they slowed down and adjusted their pace so that they weren't too close to the men, but not too far away. They didn't want to let the men know that they had company, but at the same time they couldn't afford to lose them.

Fortunately, most of the leaves had fallen from the trees which made it fairly easy to see the glow of the torchlight up ahead.

They had been following the men for roughly fifteen minutes when it started to snow. Within a matter of minutes, Joe realised that things were turning from bad to worse. If the snow continued to fall, it would cover up the men's tracks which meant they would have to walk closer to the men in order not to lose them. It might also mean that the men themselves might get lost.

As the snowflakes continued in earnest, Joe looked

at Will. "We'd better get closer to the men. We can't afford to lose sight of them."

Will glanced around at the falling snow. "No, especially in this weather." He followed Joe's lead and hurried past the bushes and trees. A few seconds later, he tripped.

"Did you hurt yourself?" Joe asked, helping Will to his feet.

"No." Will gave a sheepish grin. "Sorry about that. I was thinking about how I was going to explain this story to my dad. In future I'll look where I'm going."

"Are you sure you're okay?" Joe said.

Will nodded. He resumed walking, but stopped a few seconds later as Joe came to a halt in front of him. "What's wrong?"

"Blow!" Joe whipped his head from side to side, scanning the bushes. "I can't see the light of the men's torch."

Will pointed. "The last time I saw the light, it was in that direction."

"Yes, that's where I thought it was as well." Joe resumed walking, going as fast as he could over the newly fallen snow. As he arrived at the spot, he glanced around. However, there was still no light to be seen.

"Bother!" Joe kicked the snow in frustration. "It's my fault. As soon as it began snowing, I should have sped up."

"We might still be able to find the men." Will looked behind him and then in front of him. "We've been going in a fairly straight line, so there's every chance that the men are still walking in the same direction."

"That's possible," Joe admitted. "Come on, let's see if you're right." He set off at a jog in the direction in which Will thought the men might be.

CHAPTER 20

LOST

Unfortunately, the boys soon came to a wall of rock. Joe looked to the left and then to the right. "Which way do we go now?"

Will studied the ground to see if he could spot any footprints. But the newly fallen snow had covered any marks that might have been left by the men. He sighed. "I suppose we'll have to face the fact that we've lost them."

Joe glumly nodded. "I say we turn around and walk back to the plane."

"And do what?" Will looked to the left and then to the right. "We could take a gamble and just keep walking. We might get lucky and choose the same path that the men took."

"And what if we choose the wrong path?" Joe shone his torch around. "Even if we did choose the right direction, who is to say we'd know where to go after that?" He shook his head. "We could spend hours walking about in this wilderness and get nowhere. Besides, our torch batteries might not last for much longer. I've noticed that the light has been getting dimmer, so let's say we were to walk for another hour, we might find ourselves without a light. Then we truly would be lost in the wilderness."

"We would still have the moon," Will said.

"Possibly, but if clouds covered the moon then we'd have no light whatsoever," Joe replied. "I think the best plan would be for us to head back to the plane. I know we've come a fair way, but at least we know the direction we have to walk in. If we were to continue on, we'd probably lose all sense of direction."

Will nodded. "Okay. Let's do that."

As he and Will had been going in a fairly straight line prior to losing sight of the men, Joe felt their chance of reaching the plane before long was fairly high. But the one thing that he had misjudged was their torch. The batteries were getting low and the light getting dimmer much faster than he had anticipated.

To make matters worse, the snow was falling faster than before. Joe looked up at the sky but he couldn't see any stars at all. "It looks as though this snowstorm might continue for a while."

Will rubbed his hands together. "Yes, and it's getting jolly cold. My hands have been freezing for the last five minutes."

"Once we arrive back at the aeroplane we'll be able to warm up," Joe reassured him.

"You mean if we get back." Will stopped and looked around. "The bad thing about being lost at night is that every tree and bush looks the same."

As Joe stopped beside Will, he noticed that the torchlight had dimmed even further. "If we don't find the plane soon, we'll have to find somewhere else to spend the night."

Will suddenly rushed over to a bush. "Shine the light over here!"

Joe swung the torch in his direction and followed his friend. "What?"

Will grinned as he picked up a piece of metal. "Look!"

Joe grinned back. "That must be part of the plane."

Will nodded and dropped the object. "If we follow the trail of debris, it should lead back to the aircraft."

Joe swung the torch from left to right, hoping to spot another piece of metal. As he did so, he smiled. "Here's another one."

A few moments later, the boys had found another piece. They hurried forward, stopping when they caught sight of part of a wing.

"This must be the one that broke off." Will eagerly strode forward. "And if the wing's here, then the rest of the plane should be just a little bit further ahead. Come on, let's see if I'm right."

Joe yelled out in happiness as he caught sight of the plane's fuselage a few moments later. "Yes! We've made it."

Will sighed with relief. He gazed at Joe in appreciation. "If we had followed my plan and continued on, we'd probably still be walking about in the woods. And, with the state that the torch is in, I'm not sure what we would have done."

"Well, you're the one who spotted that broken piece of metal," Joe said. "If neither of us had spotted it, we might have walked right past the aeroplane. So it was a team effort. Come on, let's look for something warm, I'm freezing."

The two boys hurried into the cabin and shone the torch around. Joe spotted some rugs that were covering the first row of seats and hurried over. "These should do nicely."

"Let's take them all," Will said. "We can never be too warm."

After gathering up all the rugs, they spread some

of them on the seats that they had sat in earlier and covered themselves with the remainder. After saying goodnight to one another, Joe switched off the torch and placed it on the floor beside the seat.

As he closed his eyes, his thoughts turned to his sisters. He had been very much disappointed when he had found out that they had been split up but now, thinking about all that he and Will had gone through in the last couple of hours, he was glad that things had turned out the way they had. That's not to say that he wouldn't have preferred to be sitting next to the fireplace at his grandparent's farmhouse instead of in this cold and uncomfortable plane, but if he had to choose between him and Will or Amy and Sarah being stranded in the mountains, he was glad that it was the boys and not the girls.

It was one thing for them to sleep in this cold plane, but he didn't know how the girls would have coped as they were younger and were more likely to get cold during the night.

He heard a flutter of wings and, as an owl hooted in the sky above, he grimly smiled. That was another thing the girls wouldn't have liked. That wasn't the first animal noise that he had heard in the last couple of hours and he knew that it wouldn't be the last.

Try as she might, Amy couldn't fall asleep, so she sat up. Thoughts turned to how close they had been to escaping. Like the boys, she and Sarah had climbed into their crates just before the men had walked into the cave.

She had been unable to see what was going on, but from the grunting sounds that the men were making she could imagine what was going on. She was shocked, as this was unexpected, but she thought that maybe this would turn out to be a good thing.

But it hadn't. For some reason, after ten minutes, all sounds of activity had ceased. She had expected that her crate would be moved, but it hadn't. So, after making sure that the men had gone, she had climbed out of her crate.

After having no luck finding the lamp, she had called out. Sarah had responded and it hadn't taken them long to realise that they were all alone in the cave.

They had tried making their way out of the cave but, a few minutes later, they had been spotted by one of the men. Without a light, it had been impossible to escape. Before they knew it, they were taken back to the cave that they had been held in earlier.

Baldy had interrogated them, but as he couldn't get any information out of them, he had left them and gone searching for the boys. But, before he had left, he had instructed Spiky to keep his eyes on them at all times.

Escape had so far proven to be impossible as he had never left the cave. Even now he was sitting on a seat staring up at the roof of the cave. He had only spoken to the girls once and it had been brief. Basically, he'd told them that they had no chance of escaping and that the boys would soon be back with them.

Amy had hoped that the boys had managed to escape and were already on the way to the mine with the police, but as the minutes had turned to hours, she felt that they too must have been captured.

Amy had attempted to think of a plan, but had so far been unsuccessful. This was why she had decided to try to get some rest. But, after tossing and turning for what seemed like a few hours, she had sat up. She had no idea why the boss had decided not to take them to the house, which had been the plan earlier, but it was clear to her that she and her sister would be stuck in this cave for the rest of the night.

She looked over at Spiky as she heard a noise. He was snoring. A glimmer of hope appeared in her eyes. If the man was truly asleep, she and Sarah could take the lamp and creep out of the cave. She decided to wake Sarah. She hurried over and gently shook her sister's shoulder.

Sarah yawned. "What's wrong?"

"The man's asleep," Amy whispered. "This could be our chance to escape."

Sarah frowned. "Are you sure he's asleep?"

"Well, he's snoring, so—" Amy replied.

"Then let's go now before he wakes up," Sarah interrupted, standing up.

Amy put a hand on her sister's shoulder. "Let's take it slowly. Really slowly. We'll only get one chance at this."

Tiptoeing as softly as she could, Sarah followed her sister across the cave floor.

CHAPTER 21

THE DAWN TREK

As the morning sun streamed in through the aeroplane windows, Will awoke. For a moment he couldn't think where he was. Then it all came back to him. Exploring the mine, getting captured, hiding in the crates, crashing in the mountains, losing the men in the darkness, and finally spending the night in the aeroplane.

Will's heart sank as the seriousness of their predicament suddenly struck him.

He had read many stories about people going hiking and getting lost in the wilderness, never to be seen again. He quickly cast these doubts from his mind, determined that this would not be their fate.

He sat up and looked out of the window. It was a bright and sunny day. The storm clouds from the previous night had long since disappeared and there was a clear blue sky. It was the perfect day to be going tobogganing or ice skating, but instead he and Joe would be tramping through the woods. He walked over to where Joe was still sleeping and shook him. "Time to get moving."

Joe yawned and sat up. He stretched his legs, stiff from sleeping in such a cramped position. "Did you wake up during the night?"

Will shook his head. "I thought I might since I wasn't very comfortable, but I didn't."

"Me neither," Joe replied. "It must have been all the exercise that we had yesterday." He stretched his arms. "I'm hungry. Are you?"

Will nodded. "Yes. That piece of bread the men gave us yesterday afternoon wasn't exactly filling." He suddenly paused. "Did you hear that?"

"Hear what?" Joe asked, yawning again.

"I thought I heard voices." Will walked over to the window and gazed out. No one could be seen. "Maybe I was mistaken." All of a sudden, he caught sight of three people emerging from the trees. He stared in shock as he recognized Muscles and Baldy. "It's the men!"

"What?" Joe hurried over to the window and followed Will's gaze. As he saw the men, Muscles looked directly at him. The man yelled out and hurried across the snow towards the aeroplane.

"We need to get out of here now!" Joe exclaimed.

"And go where?" Will asked. "Those men can run twice as fast as us."

"We might be able to hide in the woods somewhere," Joe replied. "Come on! It's better than being held hostage again."

The boys left the window and hurried out of the aeroplane. Joe paused for a moment to get his bearings and then, spotting a thick clump of trees, ran towards them. They had just reached the shelter of the trees when another yell rang out.

As the boys raced down the hill, they were amazed to discover that, within a few minutes, thick fog had surrounded them.

"Where did all this fog come from?" Will asked, puzzled. "There wasn't any at the top of the hill."

"I have no idea, but it's a good thing for us that it's foggy," Joe replied. "It will make it harder for the men to find us." He glanced backwards as he heard footsteps. He couldn't see anyone through the fog but, as a branch cracked nearby, he assumed that at least one of the men wasn't far away. He turned to Will. "Let's find a tree and climb up it. Hopefully the men will walk right by us."

"Good idea," Will said.

It didn't take long for the boys to find a suitable tree. And it took even less time for the two of them to climb it. Once Joe thought that they were high enough, he turned to Will. "Let's stop here."

"What are we going to do if they glance up and spot us?" Will asked.

"I don't know, so let's just hope that they don't." Joe suddenly stopped. "Quiet! I think I heard someone."

~

Amy was just reaching for the lamp when Spiky stirred. She froze and so did Sarah. They waited as the man yawned. She prayed that he wouldn't open his eyes, which he didn't. After waiting a minute for the man to get comfortable again, Amy attempted to grab the lamp once more.

As her hand clasped the handle, she grinned. As she carried the lamp down from the top of the crate, it brushed against the wood and made a slight noise.

The man stirred yet again and, unfortunately, opened his eyes this time.

"Run!" Amy yelled.

As the girls tried to make their way past the man, he put his hands out and blocked the entrance. "You thought you could escape, hey?" Spiky snarled. He

130

held out his hand. "Give me back the lamp!"

Amy reluctantly handed it back. "We're just children, so can't you—"

"Quiet!" Spiky interrupted. He placed the lamp back on the crate and glanced around the cave. He spotted two coils of rope that were lying on the floor and picked them up. "Since you tried to escape, I'm going to tie you up."

"You can't do that!" Sarah shouted.

"Shut up!" Spiky yelled. "I didn't come to this mine to take care of a couple of kids, but if I have to, I'm going to make sure I do it the easiest way possible. Now, put your hands behind your back and be quiet. I don't want to hear a single sound come out of your mouths for the next few hours. Got that?"

"But—" Amy spluttered.

"Shut up!" Spiky glared at Amy and she fell silent. Both girls put their hands behind their backs and let the man tie their hands together with a rope. He then instructed them to move to opposite sides of the cave.

Satisfied that they could no longer escape, Spiky walked back to his seat and sat down.

After sitting in the tree for ten minutes, the boys climbed down and resumed walking. Silence reigned as the boys continued their descent down the mountain. Gradually, the fog began to lift and, after twenty minutes, it had disappeared completely.

As the boys emerged from a clearing and gazed down at the valley below, Will yelled out and pointed. "Look! Maybe someone lives there!"

Joe peered at the small building in the distance. "Let's go down and see."

The boys hurried down the slope. Arriving at the building five minutes later, their hearts sank. It was just a hikers hut and it was deserted.

Will sighed, disappointed. "I was hoping that there would be someone here."

"Well, this proves we're near…" Joe stopped talking as he stumbled and fell face first onto the snow.

"Are you okay?" Will asked, helping Joe to his feet.

Joe glanced down at the ground and saw a sharp rock poking out of the snow. "I think so." He resumed walking, but stopped a few moments later.

"What's wrong?" Will questioned.

"My ankle. I think I might have twisted it," Joe replied. "Let's have a rest for a few minutes."

The two boys made their way back to the hut and sat down on the bench. After five minutes had passed, Joe attempted to walk again. But he couldn't. He looked at Will. "You'll have to go on without me."

"I'm not going to leave you behind," Will protested. "That's not what friends do."

"It's the only option," Joe said. "If I went with you we'd have to go really slowly and who knows how long we'd have to walk before we found someone to help us. Besides, if one of the men spotted us, he'd be able to run faster than me."

"But—" Will argued.

"We've got to think about Amy and Sarah," Joe interrupted. "They're relying on us to contact the police. And, if both of us get captured, that's not going to happen. So we've got to split up."

"But what if I get lost and the police don't come and get you until tomorrow?" Will said. "You might freeze to death if you have to stay in this hut overnight."

"I'm sure it won't come to that," Joe replied. "I can't see someone building this hut if it were a long way from a road, so if you continue walking down the mountain I'm sure you'll find help before long."

Will peered out of the window. "What if one of the men sees this hut?"

"Then I'll have to hide in the woods until he goes." Joe glanced at his watch. "If you get going now, all this should be over soon."

"I hope so." Will opened the door and walked out of the hut.

Joe watched his friend disappear into the trees. Then, after peering through the other windows to make sure the men weren't nearby, he walked over to the bench and lay down. If one of the men came to the hut, he'd have to flee quickly, and he could only do that if he gave his ankle time to recover.

CHAPTER 22

SAVED BY THE FOG

After walking for fifteen minutes, Will was overjoyed to see a road in the distance. He hurried down the hill and sighed with relief as he stepped onto it. He looked left and right, hoping to see a car. There was none.

Deciding to head left, he strode briskly along the road. As the minutes passed, Will wondered how far he would have to walk before he came across a house.

Luckily, it wasn't long. Five minutes later, he caught sight of one. This spurred him on to walk faster. A few moments later, he spotted the roof of another house.

Will's smile widened. This looked promising. He hurried on and, as the seconds passed, he saw the roofs of more houses. He grinned. It looked as though he had reached a village.

Arriving at the main street, he hurried down it, searching for the police station. It didn't take him long to find it.

Will ran up the path and rapped on the door. "Hello!" There was no answer. He rapped again and yelled out. "Is anyone in there?" There was still no answer. He glanced at his watch and realised that it was quite early. The constable was probably still at home.

Deciding that he couldn't wait any longer, he decided to knock on someone's door and see if they could contact the police in Dunmoore. He hurried down the path and reached the road just as a cream van screeched to a stop beside him.

"Hey!" Will called out. "Could you…" He paused as he caught sight of the driver. It was Baldy!

Shocked, Will turned and ran down the path as fast as he could with Baldy and another man in hot pursuit. He spotted a side lane and headed down it, hoping to find a hiding place as soon as possible. Seeing a back garden that was overgrown with weeds and bushes, he leapt over the fence and rushed to the nearest clump of foliage. He stayed as quiet as a mouse as the two men hurried down the lane.

"Where did he go?" Baldy shouted.

"I don't know. But he couldn't have gone far," the other man replied. "Maybe he climbed over this fence."

Will didn't move a muscle as he heard the two men searching the garden. A minute later, a hand grabbed his arm. He glanced up and saw it was Baldy.

"Let me go!" Will yelled.

Baldy didn't reply as he dragged Will out of the bush. He looked at his companion. "Bring the van around."

Realising that all hope would be lost as soon as he climbed into the van, Will yelled out, hoping to attract the attention of anyone nearby. "Help! Help!"

Baldy immediately put his burly hand over Will's mouth as he made his way to the gate just as the van pulled up. He pushed Will into the vehicle and the driver put his foot down. As the van headed down the main road, he glared at the red haired boy. "Why did you try to escape? Didn't the boss tell you that we're going to be leaving soon?"

"Why would I believe what the boss said?" Will

replied. "I don't even know him. For all I know, you could lock us up somewhere and throw away the key."

"We're not murderers," Baldy said.

"Then let me go," Will said.

"No!" Baldy shouted. "Now, be quiet while I think about how we're going to catch your friend."

~

Only an hour had passed since Will had left him, but it seemed much longer. Joe stood up and tried walking again. His ankle still hurt, but it was less painful.

He walked over to the window and looked out. He wondered if Will had managed to find help yet. Spotting a movement in the trees on the slope above the hut, he paused.

A moment later, he saw a man emerge from behind a tree trunk. It was Muscles! Knowing that he had to leave the hut quickly, he made his way to the door. He opened it slowly, wincing as the wooden door gave a loud creak. He stepped out and gazed up the hill. No one was in sight. Where had the man disappeared to? Had he heard the noise of the door?

Joe didn't know and he wasn't going to stay and find out. Walking as fast as he could, he hurried into the wood, looking for a place to hide. A yell rang out just as he reached the trees and he knew that he had been seen.

Dismayed, but not willing to give up quite yet, Joe ran as fast as he could into the woods. The pain from his ankle shot through his leg and he struggled to keep up the fast pace. A minute later, he was forced to slow down, the pain was too great.

Spotting a thick bush, he hurried over and squeezed into the middle of it. Hearing the snapping of twigs and branches, he buried his head in the leaves and closed his eyes, hoping that when he opened them again, the man would be gone.

~

After driving for more than thirty minutes, the cream van came to a stop beside the same house that the lorry had parked beside the night before.

"Out you get," Baldy ordered.

Will obeyed and followed the man up the path to the front door. Baldy led the way up the staircase and along a hallway, stopping beside a locked door. He took a key from his pocket and put it into the lock. Once the door was open, he shoved Will inside the bedroom without saying a single word.

As Baldy slammed and locked the door, Will sighed and then stared in shock as he saw a figure sitting on the bed. It was Joe. Will walked over to the bed and sat down. "How did they catch you?"

"Muscles spotted the hut," Joe replied. "I tried to run into the woods, but my ankle was hurting too much so I was forced to hide. Unfortunately, it didn't take long for Muscles to trace my footsteps to the bush and, before I knew it, I was being dragged down the mountain and shoved into a car." A thin smile flickered across his face. "If I'd known the road was that close, I could have walked there myself. So, what about you?"

"I managed to come across a village shortly after I left the woods," Will said. "I was so excited, but then I discovered that the police station wasn't open."

"It must have been too early," Joe said.

"That's what I thought," Will said. "Anyway, as I was about to make my way down the street, a van roared down the road. Unfortunately, the bald man was driving it and it didn't take long for him to catch me." He lay down on the bed. "This definitely isn't how I imagined our adventure would end."

"It hasn't ended yet," Joe pointed out. "Remember the saying, it's always the darkest just before the dawn?"

Will nodded. "Let's hope there's some truth in that. Otherwise, who knows how long we'll be locked up in this house for."

~

Ever since Spiky had tied them up and instructed the girls to sit either side of the cave, Sarah hadn't been happy. Especially when he had told them that they couldn't speak to one another. She glanced towards the man as he yawned and stood up. She quickly looked away and slumped her head down, pretending to be asleep. Out of the corner of her eye she saw him grab the lamp and walk out of the cave.

Sarah had been hoping that the man would leave them and assumed that he was going to get something to eat, but she hadn't expected that he would take the lamp with him.

But he had, which meant that escape was now impossible. Well, nearly impossible. She suddenly remembered that the man had placed a torch on top of one of the crates when he had come to relieve the first man. She called to her sister. "Are you awake?"

"Yes," Amy replied. "Hey, now that the man has gone, do you think we should try and untie each other's ropes?"

"We'll need to be quick," Sarah said. "He'll probably be back soon. Shall we meet in the middle?"

"I'll come over to you," Amy replied. "Just keep on

talking so I know where you are."

"Well, do you think…" Sarah suddenly paused. "I think I just heard something."

"Me too," Amy said. "It seems to be coming towards us."

Sarah froze with fear as she heard what sounded like small footsteps coming closer. Then, as a furry animal brushed against her legs, she cried out. "It's Jock!"

CHAPTER 23

THE ROLLERCOASTER RIDE

Amy smiled in delight. "How did he manage to find us?"

"Well, Grandpa said he was an amazing dog and this proves it," Sarah said. "Hey, I wonder if he can chew these ropes off?"

"Let's see." Amy called out to Jock. "Here boy!" She snapped her fingers together. "Chew these ropes." As it was completely dark, she had no idea where the dog was but, a moment later, she felt his body brush against her legs. She then felt his mouth near her hands. She smiled as he started chewing. "Yes! He's doing it. Good boy, Jock! Good boy!"

"Hooray!" Sarah shouted. "He really is amazing. As soon as your hands are free you can untie my ropes."

"Yes, well, I've almost got them free," Amy replied. "Come on Jock, just a little bit more. There, that's done it." Amy flung the rope aside and felt in the darkness for her sister. As soon as she had found Sarah's hands, she started to untie the knots. A minute later, both girls were free. "Now, let's escape before the man returns."

"But how? We don't have a light," Sarah said.

"I'm going to find the torch that the man left," Amy said. "Let's hold hands and walk towards the crates. If we work together we'll be faster."

Sarah clutched her sister's hand and the two of them walked across the cave floor. Once they reached the crates, they moved their hands across the top of them.

Fortunately, the torch was on one of the first ones that they searched and so, a few moments later, Amy found it. She grabbed it and switched it on. As light flooded the room, she breathed a sigh of relief. "Let's go. We don't have time to waste." She hurried to the entrance of the cave. "If Jock found his way to us, he might be able to show us the way out." She looked at the brown dog. "Come on boy, show us the way out of the mine."

Jock gave a soft bark to show that he understood before he trotted down the tunnel. The girls willingly followed him. As the dog reached an intersection, the girls expected him to head towards the storage cave as they had thought that was where an exit would be, but he didn't.

However, trusting that Jock knew where he was going, they continued to follow him. He soon reached another intersection and went left this time, going down a tunnel that the girls hadn't yet explored. It didn't take long for the girls to realise that this tunnel was different from the others. After being flat for a few feet, it began to slope upwards.

After walking for a while, Sarah looked at Amy. "If we continue going uphill at this rate, we'll soon be above ground."

Amy nodded, smiling. "Yes, and it might lead to a side entrance."

As the girls rounded a corner, they stopped and gazed in disappointment as they caught sight of a sign in the middle of the tunnel. Scrawled in capital letters were two words: Tunnel closed.

Disappointed, Sarah looked at her sister. "We'll have to go back."

"Wait!" Amy replied. "Let's see what Jock's going to do." As the animal went under the sign and continued up the tunnel, she glanced back at Sarah. "That's good enough for me."

The girls continued walking, only to stop a minute later as they came in sight of a rock fall which covered the entire width of the tunnel.

"We'll have to turn back," Sarah said, crestfallen.

"Where's Jock?" Amy shone her torch around the tunnel but she couldn't see any sign of him. She frowned and called out. "Jock!"

As barking erupted from the other side of the rock fall, Sarah looked at Amy. "How did he get through?"

Amy's eyes gleamed. "There must be a hole!" She hurriedly shone her torch around every portion of the rock fall. A few seconds later, she spotted what she was searching for. "Look! That must be how he got through." She shone the torch through the hole and spotted the dog. As the light shone upon him, he barked.

"Why is he barking?" Sarah asked.

"I don't know. But if he keeps it up, the men will soon discover us." Amy called out. "Jock! Come here!"

The dog stopped barking and crawled through the hole. Once he had rejoined the girls, Amy looked at Sarah. "We'll have to enlarge the hole before we can fit through there."

The two girls set to work moving the rocks but, before they had made much of an impact, Sarah paused. "Is that voices I hear?"

"I think so," Amy said. "The men must have heard the barking."

Sarah looked towards the hole. "What are we going

to do? The hole isn't large enough yet for us to crawl through."

"Jock will have to buy us time." Amy gazed at the dog. She pointed down the tunnel. "Bark at the men, Jock!"

As the dog raced away, the girls resumed moving the rocks. They worked side by side, removing as many rocks as they could while Jock barked non stop. Suddenly, Jock yelped in pain.

Sarah swung around, concern on her face. "Oh, no!" A few moments later, the dog bounded around the corner. She quickly examined him, worried that he was injured.

"Is he okay?" Amy asked.

Sarah nodded. "I think so. I can't see any blood, so maybe one of the men kicked him." She looked down the tunnel. "I can hear voices. They must be coming up the tunnel."

"We'll have to hurry if we're going to escape," Amy muttered. "You go first."

"But I'm not sure if it's big enough," Sarah said.

"Just try it and see!" Amy ordered.

Sarah didn't waste any time in crawling through the hole and luck was with the two girls as it was just large enough for both of them. As soon as they were through, Jock crawled after them. He had just made it to the other side when the men appeared.

As Spiky looked through the hole, the girls and Jock hurried along the tunnel.

"It's not going to take them long to enlarge the hole, so let's make the most of the time we have and go as fast as we can," Amy said.

Sarah hurried after her sister. After walking for a few minutes, the tunnel widened out and a cave became visible. She stopped in astonishment. "Goodness! This cave is massive!"

"I wonder why." Amy walked around the cave, shining the torch all around as she did so. It was evident that a lot of digging had taken place, which was why the cave was so big. "I wonder how they got the gold out of this cave."

"Look! Train tracks!" Sarah hurried over to the far side of the cave.

Amy joined her and, as she shone her torch around, she saw a wooden cart. "I've read about these. Miners used them to transport stuff a long way."

Sarah put her hand on the wood and saw that it was covered with a thick layer of dust. "It looks pretty old."

"Well, the mine has been closed for over a year, so that makes sense," Amy said.

"Look! Jock is walking along the tracks. That must be way out!" Sarah exclaimed, joyfully.

Amy started to follow Jock but paused as the light from her torch lit up a ladder leaning against the rock wall. She frowned. "I wonder what that's doing there."

Sarah glanced back to see what her sister was looking at. "Oh no! The men are coming!"

Amy turned towards the entrance of the tunnel and saw a dim light that was quickly becoming brighter with each passing second. She hurried after Jock. "Come on!"

"But I'll never be able to outrun those men," Sarah muttered.

Amy slowed down and looked back. As her gaze fell upon the mine cart, she got an idea. "If we both push, we might be able to get this rolling down the slope."

"But we don't know where the tracks go," Sarah said. "For all we know, the miners might have stopped using the mine cart because part of the track collapsed." Hearing a noise, she turned towards the tunnel and saw Spiky and the boss emerge.

"We have to take the chance!" Amy rushed over to the mine cart and began to push.

"Okay." Sarah joined her and, as the cart started to roll down the slope, the girls leapt in.

Amy scanned the track ahead for the big brown dog. As she spotted him, she called out. "Jock! Come here!"

The dog bounded over and, with the help of the girls, was soon on board. As the girls turned their attention to the men, Sarah froze in shock. Spiky was sprinting after them!

As his feet pounded on the tracks, Amy peered forward, trying to see how long it would be until they reached a steeper section. Fortunately, one such section wasn't too far ahead. As Sarah cried out, she spun around just in time to see the man reach out to grab the cart.

Luckily, Jock leapt forward and bared his teeth savagely at Spiky who quickly pulled back his hand. In his haste, he failed to look where he was going and tripped.

A second later, the cart suddenly increased speed as it reached the steeper part of the track. Both girls breathed a sigh of relief as the distance between the two men and the cart increased. Then, as the cart rounded a bend, they lost sight of the men completely.

"That was close." Sarah leaned against the side of the mine cart. "Hey, this is probably what it feels like to be on a rollercoaster."

Amy smiled. "Yes. The men won't be able to catch us now."

The girls relaxed and enjoyed the ride. However, half a minute later, as the cart twisted and turned around one corner after another, they started to feel a bit sick.

"We're going too fast," Sarah said. "Put the brake on!"

Amy grabbed hold of the lever and pushed it down. She stared in shock as it broke in two. "Oh no! It's broken!"

"What? You mean we can't stop!" Sarah cried out, horrified.

"No, not at the moment, but we should slow down once the downhill slope flattens out. I'm sure there must be a…" Amy suddenly gasped as the cart rounded a bend and she saw a timber barricade straight in front of them. She froze in shock.

They were doomed.

CHAPTER 24

FREE AT LAST

Amy then realised that the track did in fact continue, however planks of wood had been nailed across the exit. "Get down low!"

Pulling her younger sister down, the two girls crouched as low as they could as they sped towards the wall of wood. A moment later, there was an almighty crash and wood splintered everywhere. The cart shot through the gaping hole and ploughed into a pile of snow.

Sarah clambered out of the cart. "I don't ever want do that again. That was far too scary and frightening for my liking."

"Well, we'll soon be back at Heather Hills and sitting in front of a warm fire," Amy said.

Sarah glanced around the snowy wilderness. "How will we find the farmhouse when we have no idea where we are?"

"Well, we're right next to Claw Mountain, so all we need to do is to follow the side of the mountain until we come to the boarded up entrance. Anyway, I'm sure Jock will lead the way back. After all, he's helped us get this far." Amy turned to Jock. "Come on boy, show us the way home."

Jock barked and trotted away. The two girls followed. After five minutes, Jock suddenly paused and began barking.

Sarah looked around fearfully. "It must be the men!"

"Possibly," Amy muttered.

"Possibly?" Sarah repeated. "Who else is it going to be?"

"I don't know." Amy looked for a place to hide. Spotting a dense clump of bushes, she hurried forward. "We'll hide here." Rushing over, she called out to the dog. "Come here Jock!"

Jock looked at Amy, barked once and ran away.

"What's up with him?" Sarah asked.

"He probably spotted a rabbit." Amy frowned as she heard voices. She looked at Sarah. "That doesn't sound like the men."

Sarah shook her head. "No, that sounds like—"

"Dad!" Amy yelled out as she saw her father, a police officer, and Jock come into sight. "Over here!" She ran towards the group. Sarah was right behind her.

Mr Mitchell smiled as he saw his daughters. He flung his arms out and enveloped the girls in a massive bear hug. "Where have you been? Your mother and I have been worried sick."

"I'm sorry Dad, really sorry," Amy replied. "But when the men locked us up in the mine—"

"Locked you up?" Mr Mitchell sighed. "Don't tell me that you've got yourselves mixed up in another adventure."

"We didn't mean to, I promise, but things happened." Amy glanced at the police officer. "Are you the local constable?"

The police officer nodded. "I'm Constable Bedford and I'm in charge of Dunmoore and the surrounding area." He took a notebook and a pencil from his pocket. "Now, what's all this about?"

As quickly as she could, Amy gave an account of what she and the others had been doing. Once she had finished talking, Constable Bedford shook his head. "I never would have guessed that someone was secretly digging up the gold."

Mr Mitchell turned to the police officer. "We need to find the boys."

"Yes, that will be our first priority," the constable replied. "Let's get back to Heather Hills. From there I'll telephone Lochnell and Castleton. We'll need their help if we're going to catch all the men."

Without further ado, the group made their way back to the farmhouse. As soon as the girls saw their mother standing by the open doorway, they rushed forward.

Mrs Mitchell hugged the girls tightly. "I've been worried sick about you." She looked at her husband. "Where are Joe and Will?"

"I don't know, but I'm sure we'll find them soon." Mr Mitchell turned to the constable. "Let me show you where the telephone is."

As the two men hurried into the house, Mrs Mitchell saw that the girls were shivering. "I'll get some blankets and you can sit in front of the warm fire. Then you can tell me everything."

~

After the four children had finished breakfast the next morning, they moved into the sitting room where the fire was burning brightly. They sat down and thought about everything that had happened in the last twenty four hours.

"I'm really sorry we got split up," Joe said. "I can't

imagine what you two went through."

"Don't be sorry," Amy said. "It wasn't your fault that the men took the crates that you and Will were in and left ours."

"I know that, but I can't help feeling somewhat responsible," Joe admitted.

"Well, at least everything worked out in the end," Will said. "If things had…" He paused as the telephone rang. "I wonder if that's the police."

A few minutes later, Mr Mitchell popped his head into the room. "That was the constable. He wanted to tell you that they've caught everyone except the boss."

"Do they have any idea where he could be?" Joe asked.

"The constable didn't say, but he seemed confident that he would be caught soon," Mr Mitchell replied.

As Mr Mitchell turned and walked away, Amy looked at the others. "He must have escaped before the police raided the mine."

"I'm not sure about that," Joe said. "I would have thought that one of the first things that the constable would have done would be to put up roadblocks on all roads leading out of Dunmoore."

"He could be hiding in the woods," Will suggested.

Sarah sighed. "If he is, he could hide out there for days and days and still not be found."

"Where would he sleep at night? It would be mighty cold if it snowed." Joe shook his head. "No, I don't think he's hiding in the woods."

"Where else would he be?" Will asked.

"I'm not sure." Joe stood up and paced up and down beside the fireplace. He suddenly stopped and looked at Will. "Do you recall the story that Mrs Olive told us about the man who shot the creature?"

"Most of it," Will said.

"What did the man look like?" Joe asked.

"He had a scar on his face," Will replied.

"And he had a limp," Amy pointed out.

Joe nodded. "Does that remind you of anyone?"

Amy looked at Sarah and then at Will. Neither of them seemed to have any idea, but then Will suddenly grinned. He looked at Joe. "You're a genius."

"Why?" Sarah asked, puzzled.

"The boss is the same man who shot the creature six months ago." Joe looked at the stunned faces of the girls. "Think about it. Whoever came up with the idea of digging up the gold in the mine had to be someone who knew where to dig, and who better than someone who had worked at the mine?"

"But if the man planned to steal the gold, why wait until just before it re-opened?" Sarah asked. "Why not dig it up after he had shot the creature?"

"Well, it would have taken time to organise things," Joe said. "Or maybe he didn't think of stealing it then. Anyway, all that matters is that now we know where the boss is hiding."

"We do?" Amy questioned, puzzled.

"Of course. He's in the mine!" Joe exclaimed. "He must know the place like the back of his hand."

Sarah frowned. "But the police searched the mine."

"I'm sure there must be some small cave or alcove that the police haven't searched yet," Joe said.

Amy suddenly grinned. "I think I know where he is."

"You do?" Will asked. "Where?"

Amy looked at her sister. "Do you remember seeing that ladder up against the wall just before we got into the mine cart?"

Sarah's green eyes gleamed. "Do you think that's where the boss is hiding?"

"What's this about a ladder?" Joe questioned.

Amy quickly explained. "While Sarah and I were being chased by the men, I caught sight of a ladder leaning up against a rock wall."

"Was there an alcove of some sort above the ladder?" Joe asked.

"Possibly," Amy replied. "I didn't have a good look at it but, if I had to make a guess, I'd say that is where the boss is hiding."

Will stood up. "Then let's go and see if you're right."

CHAPTER 25

THE BOSS

As the children and Jock arrived at the entrance to the mine, they caught sight of a police officer. After explaining their theory to the man, he agreed to accompany them to the cave.

In less than ten minutes, the group had arrived at the large cave. The police officer turned to Amy. "Where did you see the ladder?"

Amy walked over to a section of the wall. "It was over here somewhere."

"There it is!" Sarah yelled, pointing to the left of her sister.

The group hurried over to where the wooden ladder was leaning against the wall. The police officer shone his torch above the ladder and frowned. "You might be onto something. That looks like an alcove." He took out his weapon and climbed up the ladder.

The children gathered in a group with Amy focusing the torch on the ladder to help the police officer see while he climbed.

A second later, before the police officer had a chance to reach the top of the ladder, a shape loomed out of the darkness.

Sarah cried out in fright. It was the boss!

As the children watched, the man shoved the ladder away and leapt to the ground. The police officer landed on his back with the ladder on top of him. As he attempted to get to his feet, the boss zigzagged around the children and raced towards the tunnel.

"Get him Jock!" Amy yelled.

The dog needed no further instructions. He tore after the man and leapt at him, his sharp teeth making impact with the man's arm.

The boss tried to free himself from the big brown dog, but Jock had no intention of letting him get away.

By now, the police officer had recovered his weapon and he rushed up to the boss. "Hands up!"

The boss glared at the children before he reluctantly obeyed.

~

The children were having a wonderful time skating on the lake in Dunmoore later that afternoon when Sarah caught sight of Constable Bedford walking towards them. "Hey! It's the constable."

"Let's see what he's got to say." Joe skated to the other side of the lake, the others hot on his heels.

Constable Bedford smiled at the three children as they reached the bank. "Having fun?"

Joe grinned from ear to ear. "Yes, especially now that we've solved the mystery of Claw Mountain."

"Did you find out if the boss was who we thought he was?" Will said.

The police officer nodded. "Yes. He was the same man who shot the creature." He shook his head in admiration. "I don't know how you worked it out, but I'm glad you did. Oh, and so are the owners of the gold mine. In fact, they have told me to pass on a message to you lot."

"What is it?" Will asked.

"They wanted me to thank you for helping catch the men before they got away with all the gold. To show how grateful they are, they're going to give you a reward." Constable Bedford looked at the children. "You've done a grand job and you should be proud of yourselves."

Joe grinned. "Actually, if it wasn't for Claw Mountain and the mine, this holiday would have been pretty boring."

"Although it was rather scary and cold being held in the mine," Sarah pointed out.

"Yes, I agree," Amy said. "A lot of it wasn't too nice, but now that it's over, it feels good to think that we helped to catch those men."

"So, does that mean you might be coming back to Dunmoore?" Constable Bedford asked with a twinkle in his eye.

"Well, since our grandparents live here, it's quite likely that we'll be back again," Joe said.

"The snow's fun to play in, but I'd love to see it when all the heather is on the hills," Amy said.

"We can solve another mystery as well!" Will yelled.

Constable Bedford smiled. "Well, Dunmoore is a pretty quiet village, but knowing you lot, I expect one will turn up if you decide to visit again." He glanced at his watch. "I'd better get going. Cheerio!"

As the man walked away, Joe turned to the others. "I don't know about you, but my tummy is telling me that it's time to eat. How do you feel about going and buying some cream buns at the bakery?"

"Sounds good," Amy said.

"Let's just have one last race around the lake before we go," Will suggested.

Joe grinned. "Okay, I suppose my stomach can wait that long."

Everyone apart from Sarah got ready to skate across the lake and back again. Amy pointed to a bush near the edge of the lake. "You have to touch that bush and race back here."

"Fine with me," Will said.

Sarah started the countdown. "Three, two, one!" She watched as the others skated to the other side of the lake and cheered as Amy reached the bush first. It wasn't often that her sister was in the lead, and she was going to celebrate it.

As the three headed back across the ice, Joe took the lead. Will then fell, but got to his feet a moment later.

Sarah turned her gaze to her brother and sister who were still racing. Seeing that Amy had regained the lead, she yelled out. "Go Amy!"

The two were neck and neck, but then Amy inched past Joe at the last minute. As she touched the edge of the bank, her blue eyes shone. "Yes! I did it."

Joe smiled and patted his sister on the back. "Good skating."

Amy couldn't stop smiling as Will skated up to the group. "I might not be able to swim or run as well as you boys, but at least I can skate as fast."

Joe took his skates off and put his shoes on. "Come on, let's buy some cream buns before my stomach rumbles."

It wasn't long before the four children arrived at the bakery. They walked up to the counter and Mrs Olive smiled at them. "From what I've heard, you lot have been very busy since I last saw you."

Will nodded. "Yes, we found men digging up gold in the mine."

"You'll have to tell me all the details," Mrs Olive

said. "I love reading mystery books, but it's far more exciting when the mysteries are real."

"We'll tell you all about it then," Sarah said, beaming.

"Can we please order something first?" Joe scanned the shelves in front of him. He licked his lips as he saw cream buns, scones, bread rolls, and even a large chocolate cake. "I don't know what to pick. There's so much to choose from."

"Why don't we have a small portion of all the things?" Will asked. "After all, we did just solve a mystery, which isn't something we do every day."

Joe looked at the woman. "Can we do that? Just order a small portion of each thing?"

Mrs Olive beamed. "Of course. Choose a table and I'll be along shortly with the food."

As the children seated themselves at a table next to the window, Sarah suddenly pointed. "Look! It's snowing."

Amy sighed. "It looks beautiful. It's a pity we have to go back to Smugglers Cove so soon."

Joe nodded. "The one thing I can say about this holiday is that it hasn't been dull."

Amy laughed. "Are any of our holidays dull?"

"Not since we met Will," Sarah pointed out.

Their red headed friend smiled. "I must be a good luck charm." His blue eyes twinkled. "I wonder what kind of mystery we'll get mixed up in next time."

"You mean if there's a next time," Amy said.

"I'm sure there will be," Joe replied. "In fact, I'm certain of it. We might have to wait a while, but I'm sure one will come along."

Made in United States
Troutdale, OR
12/23/2023

16370875R00096